SAVING SAVVIE

BROTHERHOOD PROTECTORS YELLOWSTONE
BOOK SIX

ELLE JAMES

TWISTED PAGE INC

Dedicated to my daughter Paige Yancey for always being there when I need to bounce ideas off her to brainstorm new books. She's a sweet girl with a huge heart. Love you so much!

Elle James

AUTHOR'S NOTE

Enjoy other military books by Elle James

Brotherhood Protectors Yellowstone
Saving Kyla (#1)
Saving Chelsea (#2)
Saving Amanda (#3)
Saving Liliana (#4)
Saving Breely (#5)
Saving Savvie (#6)
Saving Jenna (#7)
Saving Peyton (#8)
Saving Londyn (#9)

Visit ellejames.com for more titles and release dates
Join her newsletter at
https://ellejames.com/contact/

SAVING SAVVIE

BROTHERHOOD PROTECTORS
YELLOWSTONE BOOK #6

New York Times & *USA Today*
Bestselling Author

ELLE JAMES

CHAPTER 1

SAVVIE SLIPPED the diamond cascade earring into her right ear, screwed the back in place and stared at her reflection in the hotel mirror.

She'd pinned up her sandy-blond hair and tucked it beneath a bleach-blond wig. The wig had been fashioned into a loose French twist with long strands hanging around her cheeks.

Expertly applied makeup made her gray-blue eyes appear mysterious and seductive. The figure-hugging black dress followed her curves, down past her buttocks and then fell softly to her ankles, effectively hiding the knife strapped to her left leg. A slit up the right side exposed her toned calf and much of her thigh. Beneath the dress, she wore a lightweight pair of black boyshort panties.

As she touched a hand to the diamond necklace

that matched the cascade earrings, she nodded. She looked like a million bucks, like she belonged in the posh Setai Miami Beach Hotel.

All part of the persona she'd assumed for this mission. Her last. After successful completion, she'd hand in her resignation and retire at the ripe old age of thirty-one. That was at least sixty-seven in assassin years. Her handlers wouldn't be happy.

If she had to, she'd disappear and create a whole new name and life somewhere in the boondocks like Kyla, who'd made it out.

Barely.

Kyla was happily living in Montana with a man who was crazy about her.

Savvie sighed.

What would it be like to live a normal life? Could she, after all the training she'd gone through to become a lethal weapon for the US government?

She'd made up her mind to leave a week ago. She was tired of being alone. Tired of always looking over her shoulder. Tired of killing, and she was determined to get out before one of her targets made a target out of her.

Unfortunately, before she could tell her superiors of her plan to leave the team, she'd been handed an assignment, briefed on the target and knew too much to say, *Never mind. I quit.*

And after reading the man's dossier, she couldn't walk away.

For all appearances, Marcus Caldwell was a playboy, living off his family's wealth via a trust fund established by his grandfather. He jetted around the world in one of the fleet of planes belonging to the family, spent his summers on the French Riviera and hobnobbed with all the uppity-ups of society.

What the people of the nose-bleed strata of society didn't know was that Marcus had blown through his trust fund by the time he'd turned thirty-five. Worse, his family had refused to pay for his lavish lifestyle and had told him to figure it out for himself.

And he had.

Within less than six months, he'd set up a corporation buying and selling high-dollar art and antiquities as a front for the exploitation and exportation of women into the sex trade.

Savvie's intelligence sources had caught him on video feeds making deals with foreign nationals known for their participation in human trafficking.

If caught in the act, Marcus's family connections would guarantee a get-out-of-jail pass, free of indictment or sentencing.

The current estimate of the number of women taken just from the US was over one hundred in the past year, with many more than that from other countries. He'd sent some of the women in shipping containers aboard cargo ships bound for Europe, Africa, China and Russia. Unfortunately, one of the cargo ships had encountered rough seas and lost a container with over a dozen women trapped inside it.

Savvie's hands clenched into fists, imagining the terror they must have experienced as they'd drowned. At the same time, they were the lucky ones to have died quickly rather than being sentenced to a living death of being drugged and raped for the rest of their existence.

Her last mission as a trained assassin was to rid the world of the monster, Marcus Caldwell.

Having been trained to maintain complete control of her emotions, heart rate and breathing, she wasn't prepared for the unexpected flutter of nerves in her empty belly.

If she believed in intuition, she'd be hesitant about this mission. As an assassin, her assignments were performed solo. On the rare occasion, she got a little help from their computer geeks, but her computer skills were as good.

Still, the fluttery feeling persisted.

Savvie frowned. If shit went sideways, she had no backup. The US government would disavow any knowledge of her mission or the existence of a government-run team of assassins.

She was on her own.

With ten minutes to spare, she paced the room. She pulled out her burner phone and stared down at it. If she could talk to anyone, who would it be?

Savvie shook her head.

No one.

Her eyebrows pulled together.

Or…maybe Kyla? Of all people, she'd understand Savvie's reservations.

It was two hours earlier on mountain time.

She entered the number she'd committed to memory and typed.

Savvie: Hey

After a brief pause…

Kyla: ?

Savvie smiled. Kyla wouldn't recognize the burner phone number.

Savvie: SS

Kyla: What's up?

Savvie: Last job

Kyla: They're letting you go?

Savvie: I'm turning in my resignation after this

Kyla: Do they know?

Savvie: Not yet

Kyla: Watch your back

Savvie: Will do

Kyla: Worried about the job?

Trust Kyla to see through her text. Savvie hadn't contacted her in months. Not knowing what to say, she didn't.

Savvie: …

Kyla: Let me know when it's done

Savvie: Will do

Kyla: GPS?

Savvie sent Kyla the map code for her location.

Kyla: Break a leg

Savvie: Thanks

Feeling a little better after her short conversation with Kyla, Savvie deleted the messages, lifted her chin, squared her shoulders and left her hotel room. She strode down the hallway in her black Jimmy Choo platform sandals and descended to the lobby.

Savvie had studied the hotel and her target over the past five nights. Like clockwork, the man arrived at the bar at nine-fifteen and ordered a bourbon neat. By ten-thirty, he'd leave with the most beautiful single woman in the place, taking her up to see the view from his penthouse suite.

Savvie had hacked into the security system and infected it with a bug that, with a signal she could trigger from her cell phone, would freeze the video feeds to display the same image for an hour. If the security team rebooted the system, the bug would bring up the same images.

An hour would be more than long enough to get up to Caldwell's suite, take him out and get the hell out of the Setai and her life as an assassin.

As she entered the bar, she glanced at the clock on her cell phone.

Nine-eleven. She had a few minutes to get into position.

She chose an empty stool at the center of the long, mother-of-pearl bar and smiled at the bartender.

"What can I get you?" he asked.

"I'm waiting for someone," she said.

He nodded and turned his attention to another patron.

People drifted in, dressed to the nines. The Bar was one of the places to be in Miami for the fashionable, wealthy and wannabes.

As predicted, Marcus Caldwell arrived wearing black trousers, a black button-down shirt open at the collar and studded with diamond cufflinks. He'd slicked back his dark hair with as much, if not more, product as Savvie had used to get her hairstyle to stay in place.

His gaze swept the room before zeroing in on the bar.

Savvie sat half-turned with her back to the bar. As soon as Marcus' gaze reached the bar, she crossed one leg over the other, the movement opening the slit halfway up her thigh.

She knew the moment his glance landed on her leg. The man's eyes flared, his lips quirked up on one side and he made a beeline for the bar and her.

Savvie pretended to look at her cell phone, watching Caldwell's movement from beneath her lashes. She didn't even look up when he stopped beside her.

He cleared his throat.

Savvie lifted her head, her eyebrows rising.

"Can I buy you a drink?" he asked.

"Why?" she asked. She couldn't be too eager, or he might lose interest.

"Because you're a beautiful woman, and I want to get to know you."

Why don't you jump off a cliff and save me the effort of killing you?

Tamping down her desire to spit in the man's face, Savvie tilted her head. "What if I don't want to get to know you?"

He chuckled. "Good point. But what's it going to hurt? And you'll get a free drink for your trouble."

"I can buy my own drinks," she said, giving him a little tug of resistance before setting the hook. "If you buy my drink, will I be obligated to answer all your questions?"

He smiled. "You aren't making this easy, are you?"

She forced a smile, hoping it looked natural. "No."

Caldwell's lips twisted for a moment as he studied her. "What if I buy you a drink and you only have to answer three questions?"

Savvie narrowed her eyes. "Only three?"

He nodded.

"Okay. I'll have the Five-star Gold Martini." She arched an eyebrow in challenge. The drink she ordered was the most expensive one on the menu.

Caldwell nodded to the bartender. "A Five-star

Gold Martini for the lady and my usual." His voice was louder than necessary for the bartender to hear. He probably wanted those people seated around them to know he was spending over a hundred dollars for a single drink.

The guy was an asshole, spending blood money on a damned drink.

Savvie swallowed bile at the thought of the women whose lives had been stolen from them by this man.

The bartender made a show of mixing her drink with Remy Martin Louis XIII Cognac and Grand Marnier Centenaire. He poured it into a gold-rimmed martini glass, sprinkled 24-carat gold flecks over the top and settled it on the mother-of-pearl bar top in front of her.

He quickly poured bourbon into a whiskey tumbler and laid it on the bar for Caldwell.

Savvie lifted her glass. "Salut."

He lifted his tumbler. "Salut." He drank his down in one swallow, set the empty glass on the bar and commanded, "Another."

After taking a small sip, Savvie set her glass on the counter. "Question number one?"

Caldwell tapped a finger to his chin. "What's your name?"

Savvie had looked up adult children of the rich and famous in upstate New York and come up with the McMadden family with their seven children.

Hopefully, he hadn't met them as Mr. McMadden liked to keep his family out of the public eye.

"Sapphire McMadden," she said. "My mother wanted to call me Diamond, but my father said it was too over the top since he owns a diamond mine." She shrugged. "So, Sapphire is what's on my birth certificate."

"Sapphire suits you. Cold stone on the outside and fire inside." His eyes narrowed. "McMadden? As in Howard McMadden?"

She nodded. "My father."

The man's eyes practically rang *cha-ching*.

"Your family is from up north if I recall correctly. What are you doing in Miami?"

"Question number two?" She waved a hand around. "Trading cold weather for sun and sand. It's May, and there's still snow on the ground in New York."

"Ahh, snow-birding." He tipped his head toward the entrance as a woman sailed in wearing a long, flowing red dress, her jet-black hair hanging down in soft waves around her shoulders. "That's Amelie Crescent, the actress."

Savvie's gaze followed the woman across the floor. Out of the corner of her eye, she saw Caldwell's hand move over her drink, shaking a fine powder into the gold flakes.

Her heart beat faster.

The bastard had spiked her drink. She imagined

that was how he got women to go with him to his suite night after night.

Well, tonight would be the last time he drugged some unsuspecting female.

"She's beautiful," Savvie commented and lifted her glass toward the entrance. "Is that Bradley Cooper?"

When he turned to look, she spilled half of her drink into Caldwell's empty tumbler and raised the rim toward her lips. When he turned back to her, she set the glass on the counter. "No. Sadly not Bradley." She giggled and swayed a little. "The drink is lovely. What about question number three?"

He shook his head. "It's my last question. I think I'll wait a little longer before I ask it."

The bartender set another bourbon neat on the bar top and removed the empty.

Savvie faked a yawn, covered her mouth and blinked. "Sorry." She smiled. "I'm not usually this sleepy."

"Are you ready for another drink?" He frowned at her half-empty glass. "Don't like the Five Star Gold Martini? I can't imagine gold flakes having much flavor."

She gave him a sleepy grin. "No, but they tickle my lips." She closed her eyes and rolled her neck and shoulders. "Is it warm in here? Or is it just me?"

"It's warm," Caldwell said. "I have the air conditioner running full blast in the penthouse. Would you like to come up with me? It has the most amazing view of the city and the ocean from the top floor."

Laying her act on even thicker, she propped her elbow on the bar and rested her chin in her palm. "I'd like that, but I'm not so sure I can make it all the way to the elevator." She shook her head, pretending to try to clear encroaching brain fog. "What did you say your name was?"

"I didn't. But your name is Sapphire." He took her arm. "Come on. Let me show you the view."

Savvie let him lead her out of the bar. "I need to use the ladies' room," she said.

"You can use the bathroom in the penthouse," he assured her.

Savvie shook her head. "Only be a minute." She dragged the words out and lunged into the ladies' room as they passed.

Caldwell tried to grab her arm before she made it through the door.

Managing to evade his grasp, she waved as she entered. "Be right back."

Once the door closed behind her, she pulled out her cell phone and touched the keys that activated the computer program that would freeze the surveillance system. Once she'd activated the code, she tucked the phone into her bra, swung back out of the bathroom, staggered and giggled. "Never mind. I can wait."

Caldwell hooked her arm and steered her toward

the elevator. Once inside, she slumped against the wall, clinging to his arm at the same time. "I don't know why I'm soooo...sleepy."

The man swiped his room card over the card reader and hit the penthouse button. "Must be the heavy gold flecks in that drink." He slipped his arm around her waist and held tight to keep her from slumping to the floor. She let her knees buckle twice on the ride up to the penthouse, making him work to keep her upright.

She didn't want to make it any easier for him.

When the door opened to the penthouse, Savvie let her target half-walk, half-drag her out of the elevator into the suite.

"I jusss...need to....sit..." Savvie let her eyes flutter closed. Not all the way. Peering through her lashes, she studied the room. Floor-to-ceiling windows gave an uninterrupted view of city lights. Nothing moved in the room. As far as she could tell, they were alone.

Good.

He helped her through the entryway and into the sitting room. Doors opened off either side of the sitting room, leading into bedrooms.

Caldwell stopped in front of a white leather couch and let her slide out of his arms onto the cushion.

Sitting gave her the chance she needed to reach for the knife strapped to her inner thigh. Guns were too bulky under a dress that hugged her body like the one she wore. And they made too much noise without a silencer, and silencers were bulky.

She sank onto the couch and slumped forward, her arm falling toward the leg with the sheathed knife. Her hand wrapped around the blade.

When Caldwell turned his back, he hit a number on his cell phone and held it to his ear.

Savvie rose from the couch in one smooth motion. She raised her hand, bringing it around the side of the man's neck. Her other hand reached for his head.

"Got a blonde. You should get a good price for this bitch along with the others," Caldwell said just as Savvie grabbed his forehead from behind and yanked him backward.

"What the—" the man gasped.

The bastard was practically counting his money over his latest female captive.

Savvie had no problem ridding the world of such a dick.

Instead of pulling forward, he backed up quickly.

Not expecting him to go backward, and wearing high heels, Savvie staggered back until her legs bumped into the coffee table. She lost her balance and fell, taking Caldwell with her.

Her back hit the coffee table.

Caldwell landed on top of her, knocking the wind from her lungs.

Immediately, he rolled to the side, twisting out of her grasp.

As Savvie sucked air into her lungs, it was cut off by Caldwell's hands wrapping around her throat.

"Bitch, my brother doesn't like it when the goods are bruised and damaged. You should've drunk the martini." He squeezed tightly. "I don't have time for this shit," he growled.

She had to act quickly before she lost consciousness. When she'd fallen, she'd let go of the knife. Reaching out, she patted the coffee table.

It wasn't there.

Gray haze crept in around the edges of her vision. She dropped her arm down the side of the table and desperately patted the floor. She touched something cool and hard. With her fingertips, she dragged the knife closer, wrapped her hand around it and thrust it upward, ramming it into his throat with deadly accuracy. The razor-sharp blade sliced through the man's jugular vein.

As blood gushed from the wound, splattering over Savvie's face and chest, Caldwell's eyes widened. He straightened and clamped a hand to his throat as all the color drained from his face.

Savvie rolled off the table and stood, wiping warm liquid from her cheeks. Movement out of the corner of her eye caught her attention.

Savvie turned to face two men emerging from the elevator.

As they rushed toward her, she shoved Caldwell's body at the man in the lead.

He staggered backward under the weight of the dying man.

A big man with a barrel chest sidestepped his partner's fall and pulled a gun from beneath his jacket.

Before he could take aim, Savvie flung her knife through the air, striking the arm holding the gun. A shot went off, missing her completely. The man's hand jerked backward, the gun flying from his grip. He cursed and pulled the blade from where it had sunk into his bicep, then lunged toward her, his eyes blazing, his lips curled back in a fierce snarl.

Savvie ran for the elevator, knowing she would have to stand her ground and fight long enough for the car to arrive and for her to get inside.

As soon as she punched the button to call the elevator up to the penthouse, she spun.

The man she'd stabbed raised the knife with his uninjured arm and jabbed it toward Savvie.

Her hand shot out, blocking the big guy's thrust. She twisted her hand, grabbed his wrist and stepped around him, bringing the wrist up between his shoulder blades. "Drop it," she said.

The man grunted, refusing to release the knife.

"Drop it," she repeated, shoving the arm higher.

His fingers loosened, and the knife fell from his grasp.

An arm wrapped around Savvie's neck and pulled her backward.

She released her captive, raised both legs and kicked him as hard as she could, sending him crashing into a wall so hard, he slumped to the floor and lay still.

The man behind her staggered backward at the force of her kick, his arm loosening slightly.

Before he could steady himself, she reached over her head and jammed her thumbnails into his eyes, digging in as hard as she could.

He roared and loosened his hold enough for her to break free.

She dove for the knife and scooped it up into her hand.

The guy still standing reached his arms out blindly, his eyes squeezed tightly shut and bleeding. "Where the fuck are you, bitch. I'm gonna kill you."

She slipped around behind him.

A bell dinged, announcing the arrival of the elevator car.

With as much force as she could muster, Savvie planted a sidekick into the blinded man's back, sending him staggering across the room. He fell over the coffee table and landed in a heap on the floor.

The door opened on the elevator as the barrel-chested man pushed to his hands and knees.

Savvie touched the button for the lobby.

Both men made it to their feet.

She held her breath, willing the door to close before they could reach her.

The man she'd stabbed straightened and shook his head as if to clear the fog.

The door slid slowly in front of her as the man lunged forward.

He was a yard away when the door closed completely. A loud thud sounded on the other side, but the door remained closed. The elevator started down the thirty-eight floors toward the lobby.

As the floors ticked by, Savvie slid her knife into the sheath strapped to her leg. Using the hem of her gown, she did her best to wipe the blood from her face. Thankfully, the elevator car was lined with mirrors. She'd only managed to wipe her forehead and cheeks clean before the car slowed to a stop. She quickly straightened her clothes and hair and reached for the cell phone she'd tucked into her bra. It wasn't there.

"Damn." She must have lost it while fighting the two men.

The car stopped on the sixth floor.

Savvie braced her legs, ready to come out fighting.

The door opened, and a young couple stepped in dressed for a night out.

The woman gaped at Savvie in horror. "Oh, my God. You have blood all over your chin and chest. Are you all right?"

Savvie gave the woman a weak smile. "It's okay. It's just a nosebleed."

Before the elevator door closed, Savvie stuck out her hand and stopped its sideways slide. "Sorry, I forgot. This is my floor." She walked out into the hallway and turned toward the stairs.

If Caldwell had men waiting near the penthouse to move their captive, he probably had men in other places around the hotel. The guys she'd left bleeding in the penthouse would have contacted them as soon as the elevator door closed.

She descended the stairs down to the mezzanine level where the conference rooms were located. She slipped into a bathroom and quickly scrubbed the remaining blood from her face, neck and chest. Without wasting too much time, she stepped back out into the hallway.

Tucked near the back of the row of conference rooms were a service elevator and another set of stairs that led to the loading dock.

Savvie hurried down the dimly lit staircase and pushed open the door leading out onto the back of the loading dock. A man wearing a shirt with the hotel logo embroidered over the pocket stood inside an office area with glass windows, looking out at the dock, an electronic tablet in his hand.

A refrigerator truck was backing up to the loading area. The dock worker stepped out of the office and crossed to the truck.

After the driver parked, he got out, climbed the steps to the dock and opened the door to the trailer.

The two men stepped into the truck.

While their backs were turned, Savvie slipped out of her heels and left the stairwell. She walked to the far end of the dock and descended the stairs, slipping silently into the shadows.

Walking quickly, she ducked between hedges and emerged on the road behind the hotel. Staying as much in the shadows as she could, she put distance between herself and the Setai Hotel.

Sirens sounded behind her, moving closer. By now, Caldwell's death would have been reported. The police would block roads into and out of the area surrounding the hotel. Caldwell's men would report that a bleach-blonde wearing a long black dress had killed their boss.

Savvie ducked into a nightclub and headed for the bar, weaving between people standing, dancing and drinking. The place was packed, and the music was so loud it pounded against her eardrums.

When the band started a different song, a group of young women squealed, and all jumped up at once from a table in front of Savvie, heading for the dancefloor.

One of the girls stopped, stripped out of a long blazer, tossed it onto her chair and then raced to catch up with her friends. The jacket slid off the chair onto the floor. As more people surged toward the dancefloor, Savvie scooped up the jacket and carried it into the ladies' room.

She had to wait in line for a stall. When it finally came to her turn, she stepped inside, closed the door and quickly stripped out of the black dress and the blond wig. When she slid her arms into the blazer, it barely covered her breasts and had only one button. She secured the button beneath her breasts, leaving her lacy black bra partially exposed and her ass mostly covered.

The resulting outfit was borderline skanky. No, it was full-on skanky. But she didn't have much choice, and it was Miami. She'd fit right in.

After removing the pins from her hair, she finger-combed the long strands down around her shoulders and used toilet paper to scrub off some of her eyeshadow.

She dropped her sheathed knife into the blazer pocket. Once she'd rolled the wig into the dress, she shoved the bundle into the container used to dispose of sanitary napkins.

A knock sounded on the stall door. "Can you hurry up in there? I gotta pee," a female voice cried.

Savvie pushed open the door. "It's all yours."

The woman pushed past her, ripping the zipper down on her jeans.

Savvie washed her hands and left the bathroom. Pushing her way through the crowd, she left the bar, skirting the dancefloor and the girl whose jacket she'd taken.

Once outside, she walked behind a small clump of guys and girls as if she was one of their group. When they ducked into a bar, Savvie kept walking north until she reached the Yucca Hotel.

Once there, she dug behind several bushes lining the building until she found the backpack she'd stashed there the day before. She slung it over her shoulder and kept moving until she found a quiet corner of an older hotel and dropped down in the shadows. Once settled, she kicked off her heels. The backpack contained jeans, running shoes, a T-shirt, two burner phones, cash, a Texas driver's license and a passport with her picture.

Savvie Sanders. She'd chosen her new identity using the nickname her friends had called her growing up in Georgia. As far as she was concerned, Savannah Johnson no longer existed.

She needed to get as far away from Miami as possible.

Her last assignment as an assassin had gone to shit. She should have known Caldwell wouldn't be alone for long.

And she shouldn't have left witnesses.

She wasn't as concerned about the law catching up with her as she was about the Caldwell family or Marcus's partners. Her handler would make sure any evidence or surveillance videos was lost or destroyed.

The Caldwells didn't forgive or forget as easily. When they encountered opposition, that opposition tended to disappear or ended up in a morgue due to a hit-and-run accident or sudden house fire.

How far was far enough?

Texas? Utah?

No. Her lips quirked up on the corners. Montana ought to be far enough.

She fired up the burner phone and dialed her handler. "It's done. Need some cleanup."

"What kind of cleanup?" a deep voice asked on the other end of the call.

"Two of his guys saw me."

"It's not like you to be so sloppy," the voice criticized.

"Yeah? So, sue me." She paused for a second. "Oh, and consider this my two weeks' notice. Make that two-minute notice. I quit."

"It doesn't work like that," the male voice on the other end of the call said.

"It's gonna have to. Don't call me. I'm done doing the big G's dirty work."

She ended the call and turned off the phone, her gut churning. Her handler made it sound like he wouldn't release her without a fight.

Since her training, she'd been more or less on her own, never coming face-to-face with the people in charge. She'd received her orders via packets she picked up at specific drop locations.

Using the second burner phone, she dialed the only person she trusted to help her disappear.

The call went straight to voicemail.

Damn.

Savvie frowned and ended the call. Instead of leaving a message, she left a text. If her friend could find a way to come through for her, she'd have to hang tight for a few hours, maybe longer. Any longer, and she'd get herself out.

CHAPTER 2

"HERE'S ANOTHER BAG." Stone Jacobs handed his fiancée a second barf bag and held her long black hair back from her face.

Normally a woman on top of her game and capable of dropping a target with a single bullet, knife, a set of nunchucks or her bare hands, Kyla Russell vomited for the sixth time since they'd left West Yellowstone, Montana, on the private jet headed for Miami.

Hunter Falcon sat as far from the pair as he could get, but it wasn't far enough to avoid the stench of bile.

"I've never known you to have motion sickness," Stone said. "And you've been over morning sickness for months. It has to be a bug or food poisoning."

Kyla shook her head. "I don't understand... I've never been sick in an airplane. Ever."

"What did you have to eat?" Hunter asked.

"The same thing as everyone else at the lodge." She stared at Hunter. "Are either one of you feeling the least bit nauseated?"

Both men shook their heads.

Stone handed her a bottle of water.

"It's just me." She unscrewed the cap and tipped the bottle up, pouring cool, clean liquid into her ravaged mouth. After swishing the water around inside her mouth, she spit it into the new bag. "I was fine when we left. It wasn't until we got into the plane and the pilot fired up the engines that it hit me. One whiff of aviation fuel and…" Her face paled even more than it had been. "I might have to drive back from Florida. I don't think I can be around that smell again anytime soon."

"It's probably morning sickness come back to haunt you," Hunter said. "When my sister is expecting, certain smells don't agree with her stomach throughout her pregnancy."

Kyla frowned. "Fuck. I swear this pregnancy is lasting forever."

"Remember that when we go for baby number two," Stone said with a quirky smile.

Kyla glared at him. "One and done, my man. One and done. I can't imagine going through this misery again."

"And you haven't even gone through the birth yet," Stone murmured.

Kyla backhanded him across his chest. "Not helping."

Stone pulled her into his arms and kissed her forehead. "Sorry, my love. Can I get you another barf bag, bottle of water or butcher knife to put me out of your misery?" He winked. "I still love you."

"I'm not convinced. I'd rather be tortured by the Taliban than be sick morning, noon and night by the smell of aviation fuel and floor disinfectants."

Stone kissed her with a loud smacking sound.

"You two need to get a room." Hunter closed his eyes and leaned his head back against the headrest. Trapped already hours in the plane, he wasn't sure he could take much more barfing or playful sparring between the boss and his lady.

Stone chuckled and pulled his very pregnant lady love closer. "Envious, Hunter? What you need is a woman in your life."

Hunter tensed, opened his eyes and shot a narrow-eyed look at Stone. "I'm content in my own skin. I don't need a woman."

Stone leaned close to Kyla's ear, the corners of his lips quirking upward. "He only says that because he hasn't met the one who will rock his world."

Kyla nodded. "Look at me... I never thought I wanted or needed a man in my life." She cupped Stone's jaw in her palm. "Now, look at me. I get all weepy when I think of you. Me! Former assassin." She laughed. "Now, a knocked-up blimp. What happened to the strong, independent and thin woman I was?"

Stone kissed her. "You're even stronger and fiercer than any man or woman I've ever known."

Kyla smiled up at him. Then her eyebrows formed a V over her nose. "But not thin."

Stone held up his hands in surrender. "I didn't say that. You're more beautiful than ever."

The thought of being responsible for a woman made Hunter's gut clench, even after all these years.

No. He didn't need a woman in his life, to be responsible for her happiness, health and welfare. He'd sworn off committing to a female, preferring to keep them at arm's length. Whenever one got too close, he walked away. To avoid being drawn into the conversation, he said, "Don't mind me. I want to get some shut-eye before we land in Miami."

"You should try to sleep as well," Stone advised Kyla. "I'm worried that flying this late in your pregnancy can be dangerous for you and the baby. I wish you'd stayed at the lodge and let us check on your friend."

Hunter had urged her to stay as well. However, Kyla wouldn't let the fact that she was eight months pregnant hold her back. He glanced at the former assassin from beneath his lashes. From the moment she'd rolled off the back of a truck, landing at their feet, she'd proven to be one of the strongest females he'd ever had the pleasure of fighting beside. She made a great addition to the team of Brotherhood Protectors at the Yellowstone office.

"I couldn't stay back at the lodge," she said. "I needed to be there. She and I went through the training at the same time. I doubt she will trust two complete strangers." Kyla leaned over, laid her head in Stone's lap and closed her eyes. "She said she'd let me know when her job was done."

"What job?" Stone asked for the tenth time.

Kyla snorted. "I told you; I don't know. Just because we trained together doesn't mean we get the same information. In fact, we weren't allowed to talk amongst ourselves about assignments. The less we knew about each other's work, the less chance of blowing someone's cover or disclosing information that could get a teammate killed or incarcerated."

"And her job is in Miami." Hunter leaned his chair back. "Somehow, I had assumed your training was for targeting dangerous foreigners. I'm uncomfortable about the fact that our government is deciding who lives and who dies among its citizens."

"They vet the targets thoroughly," Kyla said.

"Except the one you refused to kill," Stone reminded her.

Her brow furrowed. "He didn't deserve to die."

"Agreed," Stone said. "And you exposed a bad apple within your elite government-sponsored team of assassins."

Kyla's lips pressed into a tight line. "You just don't

know who you can trust anymore." She gave Stone a crooked smile. "Except you and your team of Brotherhood Protectors. I one-hundred percent trust them."

Stone lifted his chin. "Right answer."

Hunter must have dozed off, only to be jerked awake as the wheels of the small jet skimmed the runway, and the reverse thrusters kicked in, slowing the aircraft. Once they left the runway, the pilot taxied the plane to the general aviation terminal, parked and turned off the engine.

Instantly alert, Hunter unbuckled his seatbelt.

Kyla's cell phone chirped, indicating an incoming text.

"Is it her?" Stone leaned over Kyla's shoulder.

Kyla nodded, her brow dipping low. "Yes."

Hunter leaned forward. "What did she say?"

Kyla held out her cell phone for the guys to read the message.

Unk Caller: Need pizza delivery

The next text was a set of GPS coordinates.

Kyla glanced over her shoulder at Stone, a worried frown denting her smooth forehead. "She sent it over two hours ago. Nothing since."

"She's going to be okay." Stone touched Kyla's shoulder. "If she's anything like you, she's smart and good at fading into a crowd."

"She's very smart," Kyla agreed. "But why hasn't she texted since?"

"Maybe she's being followed and can't take the time to send another text." Stone unbuckled his seatbelt.

"I'm sending you both her coordinates," Kyla said.

Relieved that Stone had convinced Kyla to stay with the plane, Hunter lowered the steps and descended to the tarmac in front of the General Aviation terminal.

Stone followed him out of the aircraft and stood beside him.

When Kyla started to get out, Stone held up a hand. "No way. You're staying here. We need someone to guard the plane."

Kyla frowned. "I'm going with you."

"You're staying here, Kyla," Stone insisted. "We'll bring your friend to you."

Kyla frowned. "She won't know you. I need to be there. She might not come forward."

Stone climbed up the stairs and took Kyla's hands in his. "I know the badass in you can't stand the idea of hanging back while Hunter and I meet your friend, but think of the baby. If she's being followed, her tail will be armed and dangerous."

Kyla lifted her chin. "I can be just as armed and dangerous."

"I know you can, but we don't want to risk someone shooting at you." Stone slid his hand across her swollen belly. "Your life isn't yours alone."

Kyla's lips pressed together for a moment, and

then she sighed. "Fine. I'll stay." She frowned down at Stone. "Promise you'll be careful."

He nodded. "I will."

"If she's being followed, she might kick your ass first and ask questions later."

"We'll take that chance," Hunter said, ready to move out.

"Be sure to tell her you're delivering pizza," Kyla instructed.

"Got it." Stone pressed his lips to Kyla's. "We'll be back as soon as possible."

Hunter patted his jacket, reassured by the bulge of his handgun tucked into the shoulder holster. The nice thing about flying in a private aircraft was he didn't have to go through TSA or check his weapons. He also carried a knife in a scabbard strapped to his ankle, covered by his pant leg.

He followed Stone into the building. The brunette manning the counter smiled. "Stone Jacobs?"

Stone nodded.

She held up a key fob. "Your vehicle is in the parking lot outside."

"Thank you." Stone glanced toward the plane on the tarmac. "My woman is waiting out there. She's eight months pregnant…"

The brunette's eyes widened. "I'll keep an eye out for her."

"Thank you." Stone glanced at Hunter. "Ready?"

"Been ready." Now that they were in Miami, a

sense of urgency fired adrenaline into his bloodstream. "The sooner we find Kyla's friend, the sooner we can be on our way back to Montana."

Stone nodded. "Kyla shouldn't have come. I'm worrying about her when I should be worrying about her former teammate."

As soon as they stepped outside, Stone hit the unlock button on the key fob. Lights winked at them.

Hunter hurried toward the dark sedan parked beneath the bright glow of a streetlight. He rounded to the passenger side and slid in. Stone liked to drive, which was fine with him. It left him free to look around.

As Stone backed out of the parking space, Hunter brought up the GPS coordinates on his cell phone and locked in directions.

"If she's on the run, these coordinates could be old news," Hunter said. "Sent two hours ago, a lot could have happened in that timeframe."

"Right," Stone said. "But it's all we have for now. If Kyla gets any more information, she'll pass it on to us. In the meantime, we go with what we have."

Hunter nodded and stared through the windshield at the road ahead.

Since it was the middle of the night, the traffic wasn't bad. However, he could imagine the same roads during the day being packed.

It didn't take long until they arrived at the bridge crossing over to the island of Miami Beach.

Before they reached the other side, Hunter could see flashing lights ahead on the outgoing side of the bridge.

"It's a roadblock," Hunter said.

"If they've blocked this bridge, the others will be similarly blocked," Stone noted. "If she's still on Miami Beach, getting her off will be hard."

"By road," Hunter noted.

"Right." Stone nodded.

A spotlight shone down from overhead as a helicopter flew by.

"Do you get the feeling we should step back and maybe stay out of this?" Hunter said. "I mean, we could be aiding and abetting a murderer. What's the jail time for someone who does that?"

Stone shook his head. "I don't know. But I'm not getting warm fuzzies about this whole situation."

"Me either."

"But if we don't go in, Kyla will." Stone's jaw hardened. "I can't let her get anywhere close to this circus."

Stone slowed as they drove onto the island and turned in the direction the guidance system indicated.

At one point, a police car blocked the road.

Hunter touched the button on the side of his cell phone, making the screen go black.

As they neared the roadblock, a policeman stepped up to the window and shined a flashlight into the car. "Out kind of late, aren't you? License and registration, please."

Stone blinked up at the light shining into his eyes. "Coming from the airport. Our plane was delayed. We just want to get to our hotel and call it a night." He reached into his back pocket, pulled out his wallet, flipped it open and removed his Montana driver's license. He handed it to the officer along with the rental car packet lying on the dash.

Adrenaline pumping hard through his veins, Hunter leaned across the console, careful not to let his handgun and shoulder holster show beneath his jacket. He adopted an innocent glance and asked, "What's going on? Why all the police and road-blocks?" He figured he knew what was happening but wanted confirmation of how difficult this particular extraction might prove to be.

"A man was murdered a couple of hours ago. We're trying to catch who did it." He handed Stone his license and the rental documents. "You'd do best to go straight to your hotel and lock the door."

"Yes, sir," Stone tucked his license into his wallet and slipped it into his back pocket. "Thank you for your service."

The police officer nodded and stepped back.

Stone drove away. "It's going to be sticky."

"No shit." Hunter brought up the map on his cell phone. He had a bad feeling about the mission. But

Stone was right. If they didn't get her friend out, Kyla would do it herself. All eight months pregnant of her.

Hunter was thankful he wasn't burdened with a headstrong fiancée.

Not that Stone was complaining. In fact, Stone had never been happier to be saddled with a female. The man had a lot going on with the startup of the Yellowstone branch of the Brotherhood Protectors, recruiting talent and converting the old barn behind his father's lodge into their headquarters.

Add a relationship with a former assassin, who was now carrying their baby…

Hunter shook his head. His friend was a prime candidate for a heart attack or a nervous breakdown.

No thanks.

Life was simpler when he didn't let himself get roped into a relationship. Especially with a high-maintenance woman who couldn't take care of herself. Been there. Done that. Had the scars to prove it.

Hunter had tried marriage. Once. Liz had been beautiful, charming and so very needy. She hadn't been able to figure out how to function on her own. When he'd deployed, she'd blown up his messages with how difficult it was to live alone. She'd solved her problems by sleeping with another man while married to Hunter and living off his paycheck.

It wasn't until after their divorce that he'd realized he wasn't the least heartbroken. How could his heart be broken when he'd never really been in love with Liz? He'd never allowed himself to love her.

Why?

Two reasons.

The first being, he hadn't felt worthy of her love or anyone else's.

Second, he hadn't let her get close. He wouldn't commit to emotions that deep, never wanting to feel the pain he'd felt when he'd lost his high school sweetheart due to his inability to save her. Hunter blamed himself for Sarah's death.

History. The past belonged in the past. Hunter focused on the map and the street in front of him. They were on the main drag with all the hotels lined up on one side and the beach behind the hotels.

Hunter leaned forward. "Slow down. We're getting close to the coordinates."

Stone eased off the accelerator.

Hunter pointed to a driveway that was the service entrance to one of the hotels. The coordinates were for somewhere down that driveway.

Stone drove past the driveway and parked in the shadowy corner of a 24-hour pharmacy parking lot.

Hunter stepped out of the vehicle and joined Stone, walking along the sidewalk back toward the driveway like two guys on their way back from a nightclub, heading for their hotel.

When he neared the driveway, Hunter turned in and slipped into the shadows.

Stone followed.

He'd gone several yards, moving silently, when he spotted a dark silhouette also moving among the shadows heading toward the back of the building.

For a moment, he thought it might be the woman they'd come to get.

When the figure rounded the corner of the building, starlight revealed the figure was not that of a woman but a man wearing dark clothes and a hooded jacket.

"You see him?" Hunter whispered.

Stone came up behind him. "Yeah."

The man was heading in the same direction they were.

His gut telling him the guy was after the same objective, Hunter picked up the pace.

If Kyla's friend was at the coordinates she'd given them, she wasn't far away. They needed to get to her before the guy ahead of them did.

The man disappeared through a stand of bushes.

Hunter left the shadows, ran for that row of shrubbery and slid through a gap, emerging into a manicured walkway winding between palm trees, leading from the hotel to the beach.

Starlight found gaps between the palms, illuminating spots among the trees and decorative plants.

Their guy was ahead of them, heading toward a small hut located at the end of the garden area and the beginning of the beach behind. Paddleboards leaned against the hut wall. Lounge chairs, kayaks and beach umbrellas were stacked in neat rows.

Stone touched his arm and pointed to the opposite side of the garden area. Another shadow, too big for a woman, moved slowly through the palms.

They had more company, and Hunter had yet to see any sign of the woman they'd come to collect.

The man ahead of them approached the hut and walked among the stacks of lounge chairs and kayaks. The one on the far side of the garden closed in on the hut from the other side.

When the guy didn't find what he was looking for, he turned toward the boards leaning against the building.

Something moved behind the paddleboards.

"She's there," Hunter whispered.

The guy in the hooded jacket must have seen the movement at the same time and lunged forward.

Hunter raced toward the hut, praying they reached the woman in time.

CHAPTER 3

SAVVIE HAD SPENT the past two hours moving around the location she'd texted to Kyla, praying her friend would get her text and respond soon. Taking a taxi to the mainland was out. Police had swarmed the island. She'd overheard a couple as they'd walked along the hotel's garden path, talking about how the roads leading off the island had roadblocks set up, checking all vehicles exiting.

That had happened soon after she'd escaped the Setai.

She'd walked along the edge of the beach, looking for other means of getting off the island. A paddleboard would take too long and expose her to the police helicopter flying over the island, shining a floodlight down on the beaches, streets and ocean.

Her best chance might be to hotwire one of the wave runners chained to an excursion hut further down the beach. She'd hotwired old cars before, but a wave runner? Knowing she'd need bolt cutters to free one of the chains anchoring them to the hut, she'd picked the locks on several storage buildings and found a set of bolt cutters and stashed them beneath a bush.

With the hours passing and her window of opportunity to escape in the dark narrowing, she'd given up on hearing from Kyla. She'd taken the bolt cutters to the chains holding down the wave runners and managed, after several attempts, to cut through the metal links. As she knelt beside one of the machines, her burner phone vibrated in her pocket.

She ducked low and cupped her hand over the display screen to keep the light from shining too brightly and giving away her position. She held her breath as she read the text.

Kyla: Pizza delivery. Thirty minutes. Two pies.

Help was on the way.

Savvie released the breath she'd held, hope swelling in her chest.

Thirty minutes gave her enough time to get back to the coordinates she'd given Kyla and find a good place to hide where she could observe anyone who might come looking for her. She would expect two people.

She'd chosen to hide in the gap behind the paddleboards. She would be able to observe anyone coming through the garden or from the beach.

She'd settled into her position with fifteen minutes to spare and waited.

A couple had appeared not long afterward, coming from the hotel, holding hands.

Savvie studied them, wondering if they were the two pies Kyla had mentioned. Two people could be a man and a woman.

They stopped in the moonlight and kissed, their hands roving over each other's bodies. The man slid his hand beneath her dress and squeezed her ass.

Savvie's pulse quickened. They weren't the pies Kyla had sent. But damn, they were into each other, making Savvie's body heat while observing their passion.

Finally, they turned and headed back to the hotel, leaving Savvie thinking back to the last time she'd been with a man.

A damned long time. Maybe when she settled into her new life, she'd find herself a man-friend with benefits. She wasn't interested in anything as permanent as marriage.

Having been in her line of work, she had too many secrets to let a man that close. Sex was okay. Happily-ever-after was out of the question.

A friend would be nice.

Minutes passed with no movement in the garden or on the beach.

Savvie remained alert, her senses homing in on every sight, smell and sound.

She heard the crunch of footsteps on gravel before a dark figure wearing a hooded jacket appeared on the edge of the path, moving in the shadows, unlike the couple on a romantic stroll earlier.

The snap of a twig sounded somewhere further away.

She tensed.

If Kyla sent these guys, they'd mention something about pizza. She wouldn't reveal herself until they did.

The man in the hoodie moved through the stacks of lounge chairs and around each kayak. He looked around until his gaze landed on the paddleboards behind which Savvie stood.

She shifted slightly, bracing her legs, the fight or flight instinct kicking in.

Suddenly, the hoodie man lunged toward her. Then, another man appeared from around the side of the hut.

Savvie waited until they were close enough and then shoved the paddleboards stacked against each other, sending them slamming into the two men rushing toward her.

With her backpack slung over her shoulder, she used the distraction to leap out of her hiding place and run. The beach would leave her too exposed, so she ran into the garden, heading for the hotel. Once inside, she could lose herself in the many corridors or race out the other side and onto the grounds of the neighboring hotel. She'd visualized a number of options, walking the paths over the past few days, preparing for worst cases scenarios.

First, she had to make it to the hotel.

"Get her!" a voice rasped behind her.

Footsteps pounded the gravel behind her. More sounded in front of her.

Before she could change directions, another man leaped out of the shadows.

She plowed into the solid wall of his chest, the wind briefly knocked from her lungs.

His arms came up around her.

Another man raced past where she stood in the man's arms, and the sound of fists hitting flesh ensued, yanking Savvie out of her temporary breathlessness. She tried to pull out of the man's grip, but he held on.

When she kicked him in the shin, he cursed.

"Damn it, woman. We're here to help," he muttered. "Fuck. What was it she said?"

Savvie didn't trust him. He could be lying. Not willing to take a chance, she thrust her hands up and out, breaking his hold on her arms. She balled her fists, cocked her arm and prepared to take him on.

"Damn it," he said. "We're delivering goddamn pizza."

She'd already swung her arm when the word

pizza registered. Too late. Her fist connected with his jaw, and his head snapped backward under the force.

Pain shot through her hand and up her arm.

The man stepped back and shook his head, rubbing a hand over his jaw.

"Look out!" a voice called out.

The guy she'd hit shoved Savvie aside as a man barreled toward them.

Her pizza delivery guy bent low and charged into the aggressor like a football lineman, arresting his forward movement and knocking him back several steps.

Beyond Pizza Boy and his opponent, two other men were locked in hand-to-hand combat.

With all four men occupied, Savvie debated running while she had the chance.

Pizza Boy's opponent regained his footing and came back fighting.

Hell, the man had come to her rescue, and she'd punched him in the jaw. She couldn't run away and leave him to his own devices. What if he was knocked out or killed?

At that moment, Pizza Boy took a hit to his gut.

Anger roiled in Savvie's gut. She looked around for something she could use as a weapon. The groundskeepers did a good job of cleaning up sticks and debris. There weren't any rocks or benches that weren't nailed to the ground. Her gaze landed on a decorative metal planter filled with petunias hanging by a chain from a wrought iron pole. She lifted the chain loose from its hook. Then holding the planter by the chain, she waited for an opening.

The men fought, trading punches, moving fast. When Pizza Boy's opponent ended up with his back to Savvie, she swung the planter hard.

The metal pot connected with the back of the man's head, sending him flying forward into Pizza Boy, knocking them both to the ground.

Savvie dropped the pot and rushed toward the two men.

The man on top lay still.

Pizza Boy grunted and struggled, finally shoving the guy off him. He leaped to his feet and went to his buddy's defense.

Seconds later, they'd subdued the man in the hoodie, discovering a couple of zip-ties in his back pocket.

Savvie helped the pizza guys secure the other two men's wrists behind their backs, and they tied their shoestrings together in knots and dragged them behind the hut. Her pizza guy removed his socks and stuffed them in their captives' mouths. They wouldn't be going anywhere fast or raising a ruckus that would alert others to their predicament.

The pizza guys straightened.

Her guy, the man she'd punched in the jaw moments before, pointed to the other guy. "As I said, we're the pizza delivery guys."

Savvie nodded toward the two men. "If you're here to deliver pizza, I can guess who those two are. And if they could find me, there will be more behind them."

"We have to get you out of here," her guy said.

"How?" she asked.

"Good question." Her guy hooked her arm. His partner moved ahead of them, leading the way out of the garden and through a row of bushes onto a driveway.

They emerged onto the main road that ran in front of the hotels.

The two men flanked her as they hurried with her.

"Where are we going?" she asked.

"We have a car nearby," her guy's partner said.

"You can't just drive me over one of the bridges."

"We know. They're blocked," her guy said.

"We'll think of something," his partner said.

"Either one of you good starting small engines?" she asked.

"I am," her guy answered. "Why?"

"I have a better idea," she said.

Footsteps behind her made her look over her shoulder.

"We're being followed," her guy said. "One guy."

"And there's a vehicle not far behind him," Savvie said. "How far to your car?"

"Less than a block," her guy answered.

"You won't get me off the island in a vehicle." She touched her guy's arm. "I have another idea."

"Which is?" her guy asked.

"Wave runner," she said. "Back on the beach. Just have to get it started."

Her guy's lips quirked. "I could do that."

"That might work," his partner said. "I can distract our tail while you two make a run for it. But you need them to think you're with me in the car."

"The old in-one-side-out-the-other routine, huh?" her guy asked with a grin.

"Yup," his partner spoke softly. "When I get off the island, I'll head south."

"Great," Savvie whispered. "We'll text our location when we make landfall on the mainland."

"Ready?" his partner prompted.

"Ready," her guy answered.

"As I'll ever be," Savvie agreed.

Her guy touched her arm and whispered, "Run."

As one, they took off.

When they reached the car in the parking lot, her guy's partner flung himself into the driver's seat and started the engine.

Savvie yanked open the back door, dove in, and crawled to the other side. She pushed open the door, rolled out onto the ground and ducked through a row of oleanders.

Her pizza guy was right behind her, kicking the car door closed.

As soon as he made it through the oleanders behind Savvie, his partner spun out, leaving the parking lot.

Savvie lay low to the ground, peering through the bushes at the parking lot.

The man who'd been on foot ran into the parking lot, turned and waited for a vehicle to come to a stop beside him. He jumped in, and the vehicle took off after the decoy car.

"Will he be all right?" Savvie asked.

"Stone is a smart man. He'll lead them right to the roadblock. When the police search the car, the guys behind him will see you're not in it." He stood. "Come on, we need to hurry if we want to beat the daylight."

After one more glance, Savvie rose and led the way back to the beach, where she'd cut the chain securing the wave runners.

She knelt on the beach beside the man as he pulled open the engine compartment. "Stone's your partner's name. I can't keep thinking of you as the pizza boy."

He chuckled. "Pizza boy, huh?"

She shrugged. "Or the guy I punched."

He worked his jaw back and forth as he ran his fingers inside the engine compartment. His hand stopped. "Well, talk about luck." He pulled his hand out. On the end of a string was a key. "This will be easier than I thought. Now all we have to do is push it to the water."

He rose to his feet. "You want to steer while I get behind it and push?"

She leaned over the machine and grabbed the handgrips.

"My name's Hunter," he said softly as he passed her to crouch behind the wave runner. "Ready?" he said in a hushed tone.

"Yeah."

He pushed from behind.

Savvie steered and pushed. Together they got the machine to the water.

Hunter held it steady. "Ever drive one of these?"

She nodded. "Once. On a lake."

"Unless you really want the pleasure, I'll drive." He slung his leg over the seat and waited for her to get on behind him.

She slipped onto the machine, her legs and body sliding up against his.

He was all hard muscle and strength.

With her lady parts pressed against him, something stirred inside Savvie. This was a man who could hold his own against her. She wouldn't easily intimidate someone like Hunter. She wouldn't consider many of the men she'd met as her equal or even close.

He paused with his hand on the key. "You know my name," he said. "All I know about you is that you're a friend of Kyla's from her trainee days. And yes, we know what she did and what you were trained to do. Should I be concerned?"

Her chest tightened. He'd just reminded her that her past would always be a barrier to living a normal life. Her heart hardened. "Are you concerned about Kyla?"

"Not at all. She's one of the team."

"Is she still working her old job?"

He snorted. "Not hardly. She's full-time with the Brotherhood Protectors, working with their computer guru. And she's very pregnant."

"She left the organization because she wanted to start over."

"As so many of us have," he said.

"I quit my job tonight," she said as she wrapped her arms around his waist. "My name is Savvie. All I want is to start over and live as normal a life as possible."

"Well, Savvie, when you figure out what normal is, let me know." He started the engine. "I've been chasing normal since I can remember and still haven't figured out what the hell it is. Hold on, sweetheart. It's going to be a rough ride."

When she'd quit her job, Savvie had fully expected it to be a rough ride and had anticipated doing it alone.

Reaching out at the last minute to Kyla had been spontaneous. She hadn't planned on involving anyone else in her transition. Her training with the organization had taught her to rely on herself. No one else.

She believed one of the main reasons she'd been recruited in the first place was because she was a loner—a loner who had killed her stepfather in self-defense and in defense of her mother.

Yes, she'd been acquitted, but anyone who'd known her and what she'd done would always wonder if she had it in her to do it again. Having killed a man changed a person forever.

The agency had figured she had nothing to lose that she hadn't already lost.

So, she was in for a rough ride?

All she had to say to that was…

Define rough.

Savvie tightened her hold on Hunter's middle and hung on.

CHAPTER 4

Hunter took the wave runner out far enough that the helicopter wouldn't spot it from the air. Then, he swung toward the southern end of the island.

Savvie held on tightly around his waist as they skimmed across swells and some white-capped waves.

He found he liked how her body molded to his, leaning when he leaned, their movements like one.

The woman was strong, determined and fearless.

He found himself wanting to know more about her. Mostly, he wanted to know what made someone as beautiful as Savvie become an assassin and where would she go from here?

Though his thoughts swirled around the woman pressed against his back, he maintained situational awareness, looking ahead for boat lights, determined to steer clear of harbor police and coastguard vessels. He stayed well out to sea.

All the while, he kept the lights of Miami Beach in sight until they rounded the pier at the southern tip of the island, skimmed past another island and turned toward downtown Miami.

Hunter aimed for what he thought might be a park, knowing most boat docks would have security cameras and locked gates. He drove the wave runner up onto a narrow sliver of sand and shut off the engine, glad they'd had enough fuel to make it as far as they had.

Savvie hopped off and stretched.

He missed her arms around him and the warmth of her body.

Hunter pulled out his cell phone and sent their location to Stone.

Moments later, he received a response.

Stone: ETA ten mikes

"Apparently, he wasn't delayed at the roadblocks," Hunter commented as he showed the text to Savvie.

She nodded, her lips pressed tightly together. "That's good news in an otherwise shitshow of a night."

Together, they pushed the wave runner up into the shelter of the trees. Once they'd hidden their escape vehicle, they made their way through the park, past picnic tables and a playground to the street on the other side.

Hunter stopped in the shadow of a tree where they could see the street, but others wouldn't see them. He was soaked through to his skin and sticky with salt water. Thankfully, he'd packed a change of clothes in the backpack he'd left aboard the plane.

Savvie paced within the shadows, her jeans and T-shirt clinging to her body. She ran her fingers through her damp hair in an attempt to comb through the tangles. Finally, she gave up with a sigh and stood still, staring at the road. Whenever a vehicle passed, her body tensed. She looked ready to run.

A Miami police car slowed in front of the park.

Hunter's breath caught and held.

He and Savvie remained perfectly still, knowing any movement might draw attention to the shadows beneath the tree.

After an agonizingly long moment, the patrol car drove on.

Savvie's shoulders sagged.

"Who was he?" Hunter kept his voice low enough that if she didn't want to answer, she could pretend she hadn't heard him.

Silence stretched between them.

He figured she didn't want to answer the question or wasn't at liberty to share that information.

"Marcus Caldwell," she finally said. "A trust-fund prick who ran out of money and went into human trafficking to fund his playboy lifestyle." She shook her head. "I shouldn't have contacted Kyla."

"She was coming whether you'd texted her your location or not." He chuckled. "Stone barely got her to stay put and let us go in without her."

"I didn't know she was pregnant. I'd have found a way out."

"Probably, but you had a lot of people looking for you. Law enforcement and others." He leaned against the tree and studied her silhouette. "Were those some of Caldwell's thugs?"

Savvie shrugged. "Probably. His family is Miami's mafia. They believe in retribution, no matter how deplorable the family member has become. My error was being seen. I got sloppy."

"How so?"

"I was supposed to go in, drop him and get out. Only I let him get the upper hand. It took me longer to drop him when he had me by the throat, choking the living daylights out of me." She raised her hand to her neck. "Damned sloppy. It gave his two transfer agents—aka thugs—time to get to the penthouse."

"I'm surprised you made it out."

"Yeah. Me, too," she said, her tone matter-of-fact. Any other woman would have been traumatized by the evening's events.

No, any other woman would have succumbed to the drugs and been carried out by Caldwell's thugs.

"Where to from here?" he asked.

Savvie shrugged. "I'd planned to retire and take up knitting or fishing in a small town no one's ever heard of. Maybe get a normal job that doesn't involve the lethal use of guns and knives."

"Sounds..." He tilted his head.

"Boring?" She laughed. "I could stand boring."

"How..." Hunter struggled for the right words.

"How did a girl like me get into a profession like this?" She shook her head. "I wanted to join the military, but my juvenile record held me up at Military Entrance Processing Station."

"MEPS," Hunter said. "I'm familiar."

She turned toward him. "Prior military?" she asked.

"Army. Thirteen years."

"That's a lot of years to walk away from," she noted.

"Eleven deployments in the last six years."

She shot a glance in his direction. "Special operations?"

"Delta Force."

"The best of the rest," she said softly.

"That was the sales pitch I bought into." Hook, line and sinker. He'd worked hard to get in and trained hard to stay alive.

"Specialty?"

"Sniper."

"Then you know what it's like to put a target on a living, breathing human." She spoke so softly he had to lean closer to hear her words.

He did know.

She faced the road again. "I bet your family got tired of you being away from home."

"No family. No home." He'd sold the house and given Liz all the money in their account, plus the furniture in the divorce. "I wasn't stateside long enough for any kind of commitment."

"Then why leave the Army?" she asked.

"We lost so many of our own. Men I considered brothers. I didn't see that anything we did made a difference. I'd take out a Taliban leader, and five more took his place."

She nodded. "Doesn't give you much hope for humanity, does it?"

"No, it didn't. But I'm not ready to give up on mankind. Doesn't sound like you're ready to give up, either."

"I'm hoping a different career path will help change my outlook," she said. "If I get the opportunity to try."

"Worried about the Caldwell mafia?"

"For sure." She wrapped her arms around her middle. "And maybe others."

"From prior…"

"Hits?" she offered.

His lips twitched. "I was going to say missions."

"Possibly," she said. "I expect some opposition to my retirement."

"You mean your organization turning on you?" he asked.

"It happened to Kyla."

"From what we discovered, a bad agent was involved in her case."

"There was. But who's to say he was the only one?" She rolled her neck and shoulders. "Aside from a bad agent, the powers that be in my chain of command might not let me go because I know too much about some unsolved murders of domestic and foreign individuals. If I talk about a secret US government-run organization playing God and determining who gets to live and who dies, they won't be happy." She rocked back on her heels. "Surely they realize I can't spill the beans on any of those targets, or I could go to jail for murder."

"Unless you go for a plea bargain. A get-out-of-jail-free card for information about the people calling the shots."

"They'd have the court system in their pockets."

"But not the media."

Savvie sighed. "I don't want to blow up the internet in an exposé about a secret organization of assassins. I want out of the drama and away from this way of life. I want to fade into the background."

"Sweetheart, you're too pretty to fade into any background."

She turned to face him, her eyebrows forming a V

over her nose. "Did that punch to your jaw rattle your gray matter?"

He grinned. "Not actually. It reminded me to appreciate the finer things in life."

"Like yachts and expensive vacations?"

"No," he said. "Like a colorful sunset, a drive through the Rocky Mountains after a rain shower and a beautiful woman with a killer right uppercut." He rubbed his jaw, wincing when he touched the bruise.

"Sorry," she said. "For all I knew, you were just another one of Caldwell's minions."

"I get it. I don't hold a grudge." He studied her for a moment. "I know you want out of the organization, but what baffles me is how you joined it in the first place. You were about to tell me when you were discussing your experience with MEPS.

Savvie stared at the road as if looking ahead took her into the past. "You know how they check your physical and mental capabilities?"

He nodded.

Savvie wrapped her arms around her middle, holding tighter. "They performed a background check on me and dug up some information that concerned them enough to deny my entry into the Army. I was told to pack my shit and go home."

Hunter frowned, wanting to know what information they'd discovered about her. He didn't ask, didn't offer his opinion or advice. Instead, he waited for Savvie to continue.

"I was sitting in the small briefing area where they'd informed me I wasn't a good fit for the Army when a man in black jeans and a dark leather jacket strode in, questioned me for a few minutes about my past, my desires for the future and my ability to follow instructions. He left for a few minutes. When he came back, he offered me a position in his organization."

"Did he tell you what that position would be?"

She stiffened. "I didn't care. If it got me out of my hometown, that's all that mattered. I didn't have a college education. Not that it mattered. A background check would have red-flagged me for any potential employer. The military was really my only hope. And then it wasn't." She drew in a deep breath and let it out slowly. "I took the only job offered to me. If not for rooming with Kyla during our training, I might not have even gone as far as I did."

Hunter wanted to know what in her past had made her basically untouchable. He wouldn't ask. She'd been through enough in the past few hours. If she wanted to share that information, she would.

She half-turned toward him. "You want to know what was so bad the Army wouldn't take me, or a background check would red-flag me for other employment, don't you?"

"It's not my business," he said. "You don't have to tell me anything."

"You deserve to know what kind of person you risked your life and that of your partner to save today." Her chin lifted. "The background check revealed that I had been charged with a major crime. Though I was only seventeen at the time, they tried me as an adult."

Hunter pushed away from the tree, his brow furrowing. "What crime?"

She met his gaze unflinchingly. "Murder."

Considering she was an assassin, her announcement didn't shock him as much as he thought it should. He kept his expression poker straight. "And did you commit the crime?"

"Did I kill someone?" She snorted. "Yes."

"Was it murder?"

"Some said it was," Savvie said. "I didn't care at the time. The man had to die."

"Another Marcus Caldwell?" Hunter asked.

"Worse." Her shoulders squared, and her chin rose an inch. "He was a man who'd sworn to love, honor and cherish my mother until death. She just didn't consider death would be the better choice until he made her wish for it."

Her words made Hunter's heart tighten painfully. No one should have to endure a life with such abuse. "Sounds like your mother was miserable."

"My stepfather had beaten her so many times and

told her she was nothing and couldn't get a job even if she wanted one. She was broken mentally and physically. The last time he hurt her, I snapped. The only way to keep a man like that from hurting someone you care about is to stop him for good." She stood before Hunter, chin held high. "I killed him. And I'd do it again, only a lot sooner."

Hunter wanted to reach out to her, pull her into his arms and hold her. If he could, he would take away her pain and the bad memories. He'd only just met her, but the depth of what he felt at that moment gave him a connection with Savvie he couldn't explain and made him want to protect her from anything like that ever happening again.

She frowned. "Look, I didn't tell you all that for your sympathy. I'll knock you on your ass if you say you're sorry for me. I only told you because you have the right to refuse to help me. If you walk away, I'll understand. In fact, you and your friends should leave me and forget you ever helped me escape on a wave runner."

"Not gonna happen," Hunter said.

"I'll never forgive myself if Kyla or her baby is hurt because of me." She bit her bottom lip. "I can't believe Kyla's pregnant.

Savvie swiped at her cheeks. "She's the lucky one," her voice cracking. "Out of the business. A man who clearly loves her and a baby on the way. Her life couldn't get more perfect."

In the past, Hunter had never considered all those things adding up to perfection and happiness. Now, as he recalled the way Stone and Kyla looked at each other or her swollen belly, it was clear to all that they were happy, smitten with each other and the baby.

Something tugged at Hunter's gut he'd never experienced before. For a brief flash, he wondered what it would be like to have a strong, loving woman by his side and a baby on the way. His gaze fell on Savvie, a resilient, determined individual capable of standing on her own and fighting her way out of a bad situation.

The headlights heralded the approach of a vehicle on the road in front of them. The bright lights blinked on and then off as the dark sedan rolled into view.

Savvie backed away, easing her body behind a tree trunk.

"That will be our ride," Hunter assured her. "I recognize the rental car." He held out his hand. "Let's go."

When she laid her hand in his, an electric current zinged up his arm and spread throughout his body. The shock was so unexpected he almost pulled free of her grip. But he didn't. He liked how her hand fit in his. Hers wasn't a tentative, weak grasp. It was strong, like everything else about her.

They hurried toward the sedan.

Stone lowered the window. "Get in," he urged. "I

might have a tail. I noticed him several blocks back." He glanced into the rearview mirror. "I could be wrong. He's not there now. But it's better to err on the cautious side."

Not taking time to round the vehicle to the other side, Hunter dove into the back seat after Savvie.

Stone hit the accelerator before Hunter closed the door behind himself.

After pushing himself upright, Hunter glanced through the rear window. No lights shone behind them.

Stone drove several blocks and stopped at a red traffic light.

An SUV slowed as it approached the intersection from the right.

Their light turned green. As Stone pulled forward, the vehicle on the right leaped forward, slamming into the side of the sedan.

Hunter's shoulder hit the door, his body cushioning Savvie's as she flew across the back seat.

Stone cursed and hit the accelerator hard. For a moment, the tires burned against the pavement, turning the sedan and SUV as one. When the sedan broke away from the SUV's bumper, Stone swerved and raced away, turning right onto the next street. Two blocks later, he swung left, skidding sideways into the turn.

Savvie scooted across the seat and secured her lap

belt and shoulder harness. Hunter did the same, turning sideways to look out the back of the car.

For the next few blocks, zigzagging through the city streets, no headlight appeared behind them.

Had they lost the tail?

A red traffic light loomed at the next intersection. Stone slowed well ahead of the signal. The huge office building to his right blocked his view around the corner. Streetlights shone brightly. If another vehicle were coming from the side streets, they wouldn't see them until they reached the corner.

"Hold on. I'm not stopping," Stone stomped the accelerator. The battered sedan leaped through the intersection.

The SUV with the crumpled bumper lurked beside the office building. As soon as the sedan entered the intersection, the SUV raced forward. But not soon enough.

Stone made it through the intersection, the SUV missing them by just a few inches.

"They know where we're going to be," Hunter said. "They have some kind of way of tracking us." He looked to Savvie. "Do you still have your cell phone?"

She nodded. "I have two burner phones."

"Everyone, pitch your cell phones," Stone said, "and anything that might be traced."

Hunter pulled out his SIM card and did the same for Stone's device.

Stone pulled behind a building and stopped close to a big trash container.

Hunter collected Savvie's burner phones, his and Stone's phones, and tossed them into the bin.

When he was back in the sedan, Hunter leaned toward Stone. "What about this vehicle?"

"Not sure how they'd track it, but anything's possible," Stone said. "We need to ditch it before we head to the airport."

Hunter glanced back. "I don't see headlights."

Stone kept driving through downtown Miami, making random turns, cutting back, and then moving forward. Finally, he pulled into a garage and drove to the second floor before parking the sedan.

"We need to move quickly. I'm worried they'll trace the rental car's license plate back to the airport," Stone said.

"We can catch a cab at one of the hotels."

They abandoned the rental car and took the stairs down to street level.

Moving down the back alleys and keeping to the shadows, they made it to a hotel, stepped inside and asked the front desk to call a cab. Ten agonizing minutes later, they were on their way to the general aviation airport, where the plane and Kyla waited.

Hunter kept glancing over his shoulder, looking for vehicles following them.

Stone kept looking over the driver's shoulder. "Could we go a little faster," he urged the man.

"Can't," the guy responded, maintaining the exact speed as indicated on the signs they passed.

"I'm sorry." Savvie sat between the two men in the back seat. "I shouldn't have gotten you all involved. If anything happens to Kyla…" She shook her head.

"She shouldn't have come," Stone said through tight lips. "I shouldn't have let her."

"Everything's going to be all right," Hunter said, though his gut was telling him something else. But it did no good to worry about something that may or may not have happened.

The three of them sat tense the entire drive to the airport.

"I'll go through and have the clerk open the gate so we can drive right up to the plane. The fewer people who see our additional passenger, the better."

Savvie bent over, ducking low in her seat.

Stone tossed a hundred-dollar bill over the driver's shoulder. As they pulled in front of the FBO, he didn't wait for the vehicle to come to a complete stop before he leaped out and ran for the entrance.

The driver rounded the side of the building and waited at an automatic gate. When it slid open, he drove through.

Stone stood on the tarmac where the plane should have been.

Hunter's heart flipped. "Stay down," he said to Savvie. Then he got out of the vehicle and approached Stone.

"I think I aged twenty years." Stone shoved a hand through his hair. "The clerk said Kyla came in and let her know the pilot was going to perform some touch-and-goes. I imagine she didn't want to stand still waiting for someone to hijack the plane. Apparently, they've just landed and are taxiing over. There it is now, thank God."

The small jet rolled toward them, coming to a stop several yards away from the two men and the waiting taxi.

Once the steps were lowered, Stone was first inside. Hunter had the taxi driver pull up next to the plane. When the vehicle came to a standstill, Hunter held the door open for Savvie and closely followed her up the steps, blocking her body with his.

The taxi left the tarmac through the gate and disappeared.

Once inside, Hunter pulled the steps up, and the plane left the FBO, moving onto the taxiway.

Hunter sat in the seat beside Savvie.

As the plane sped down the runway, she reached for his hand and held it tightly until the wheels left the ground and the aircraft climbed high above Miami.

Finally, she turned away from the window and stared down at their joined hands.

"No matter how many times I've been up in planes, the take-offs and landings always make me nervous." She smiled up at him. "Thank you."

"Any time," he said, reluctantly releasing her.

She glanced across the cabin to where Stone and Kyla sat holding hands.

Kyla rubbed her free hand across her belly. "Girl, I was so on edge, I thought I'd birth this baby a month early." She smiled and patted Stone's hand. "No, really. I'm fine. The baby's fine, and now you're fine."

Savvie gave Kyla a crooked smile. "It's good to see you, Russell."

"Back atcha, Sanders." Kyla lifted her chin. "What the hell kept you all so long?"

Hunter exchanged a glance with Stone and met Savvie's gaze briefly.

"Things got complicated," Savvie said.

An understatement, in Hunter's mind. And if his gut was on target, things would only get even more complicated.

"Whoever was after Savvie had resources capable of finding her," he said. "I don't think they'll give up easily."

He reminded himself that she was an assassin. Someone who killed people for a living. If push came to shove, she could take care of herself.

Yet, beyond her strength and training, there was something else that drew him to her. He couldn't quite put his finger on it.

Having just gone through the effort of saving her, Hunter wasn't ready to walk away.

CHAPTER 5

Savvie slept three of the four-hour flight to Montana, waking when the wheels touched down at the West Yellowstone regional airport.

The sun had just eased up over the horizon like molten lava. A bright orange ball of flame brightening the sky with each passing minute.

When the plane stopped, Hunter left his seat to open the hatch and lower the steps.

He stepped aside, allowing Stone to descend first and then help Kyla to the ground.

"I could do this much easier if I could actually see my feet," Kyla grumbled.

"I know you like your independence," Stone said, "but let me help. It makes me feel like I'm a part of this pregnancy, even though you're doing all the work."

"Fine. I'll let you help as long as you promise to

get me some food." Kyla stretched her arms in the air and then rubbed her hands over her belly. "I'm so hungry I could eat half a side of beef."

"If you're not too tired, we can stop at the diner on the way through town," Stone suggested.

Kyla glanced at Savvie as she climbed down from the plane. "Hungry?"

Savvie's stomach rumbled, and she laughed. "I guess that answers your question. I haven't eaten since I had a cup of yogurt yesterday morning."

Kyla nodded. "I couldn't eat much the days I worked missions. I didn't want my body working on digestion when I needed all my focus on the task ahead."

Savvie felt the same. Being focused and aware of her surroundings at all times had kept her alive. When she lost focus, she got sloppy. Like almost letting Marcus Caldwell choke her to death. The only good thing about what had happened was that Marcus's death, which should have been a targeted assassination, aka murder, ended up being self-defense.

Stone hooked his hand around Kyla's elbow. "I could use a strong cup of coffee."

He led her toward a building on the east side of the runway. As they passed through it, Stone waved at the young woman behind the counter. "Good morning, Lily."

"Welcome back, Mr. Jacobs, Ms. Russell." The woman smiled and waved.

"Thanks." Kyla smiled. "It's good to be back, even though we weren't gone long."

"Not much longer until that baby gets here, is it?" Lily asked.

"Not soon enough." Kyla lifted her chin. "When are you headed off to college?"

"Not for another month," the brunette grinned. "Maybe you'll have that baby while I'm still here."

"I hope so," Kyla said. "Did you get all the classes you wanted?"

Lily nodded. "Thanks for helping me go over the schedule and lay out my degree requirements. It all seemed so confusing. Now, I can see a clear path to getting my degree."

"Glad to help," Kyla said. "Just promise me you'll stick with it and see it all the way through."

Lily held up a hand. "I promise. I wouldn't have even considered going to college if not for you and Mr. Jacobs. Now, I can't wait."

They continued through the building and out the other side to a parking lot.

Stone stopped beside a black SUV and opened the passenger door for Kyla, handing her up into the seat. When she was settled, he stepped up on the running board and secured her seatbelt over her lap and beneath her baby bump, stopping to plant a kiss on her lips.

Savvie couldn't help but stare at the couple.

Kyla, the most driven female in her training class, who could take down any of her classmates, male or female, seemed to be an entirely different person now.

And there was no denying that she was completely in love with Stone, and he with her.

Savvie wondered what that felt like. She'd never bought into the whole concept of love.

Lust, yes. The internal chemistry that drove the urge to fornicate was built into the DNA of every living creature.

But love?

She'd considered it a fantasy marketed to the masses to sell romance movies, valentines, jewelry and expensive weddings.

Her mother had claimed she'd fallen in love with the handsome Ralph Welch, dragging her teenage daughter into a marriage from absolute hell. The man had promised to love, honor and cherish her mother. He had done all that in the beginning, hiding his true colors.

Her mother had been so happy, thinking Ralph loved her, and they'd live their own happily-ever-after like in the fairytales.

It had all been a lie. Love was supposed to be kind and caring, like in the Hallmark movies. Her mother's love had been painful to herself and Savvie.

When things hadn't gone the way Ralph thought

they should, he got mad and took his anger out on his wife and stepdaughter. He started out yelling at them. The yelling progressed into slapping. Eventually, he'd used her mother as a punching bag and almost beat her to death.

"Savvie?" A hand touched her arm.

She flinched and turned sharply to defend herself, her pulse racing.

Hunter stood there with his hands raised. "I'm sorry. I didn't mean to startle you."

She stared at him for a long moment, pulling herself back from the past to the present. "I guess I'm still a little punchy."

He stood beside the SUV and waved a hand toward the open door. "After you."

As she moved past him, her shoulder brushed against his chest, sending a spark of awareness through her.

There it was. That feeling that made her core heat and her body crave the carnal pleasures that ultimately resulted in procreation.

Lust.

She'd felt it when she'd had her arms wrapped around his middle and her body pressed to his as they'd ridden the waves off Miami Beach, the wild, untamed ocean as primal as those natural urges coursing through her veins.

The man was a fine specimen of the male gender.

Savvie could imagine having sex with him. It

would satisfy her body's needs. Lust and need weren't love.

Love didn't exist.

As she settled into the seat behind Kyla, she couldn't help but notice her former classmate was holding Stone's hand and smiling into his eyes.

How long would it be before the pair realized love was an elaborate hoax? Kyla was a smart woman. She'd figure it out soon. And then what?

More marriages ended in divorce than seeing it through to the death-do-us-part conclusion.

Savvie's chest tightened. How sad for their child. Divorce left casualties in its wake, no matter how hard a parent tried to shield her child from the aftermath.

For years, Savvie had blamed herself for her parents' divorce. At first, she'd blamed herself for her stepfather's wrath. After Ralph nearly killed her mother, she'd blamed Ralph. She couldn't have done anything differently to make him nicer to her mother. She'd learned that some people were bad and not redeemable.

That experience had made her life as an assassin easier. She'd studied her targets. Each one had irredeemable flaws that caused harm and death to others. The only way to keep them from continuing to hurt people was to eliminate them.

Hunter settled in the seat beside her and leaned close. "Are you okay?"

"Of course," she answered, once again pulling herself back to the present. She hadn't reminisced this much ever. Why was she doing it now? "I'm just tired."

"After breakfast, we'll go to the lodge. Stone's father will fix you up with a room."

Savvie sighed. "Thanks. Hopefully, I won't impose for too long. Now that I'm unemployed, I need to figure out my next career and place to live."

"Did you have an apartment somewhere?" Hunter asked.

Her lips twisted. "I did back in Virginia. I rented a one-bedroom furnished apartment over a garage. I was rarely there. The old woman who rented the apartment to me didn't care as long as I kept it clean and didn't have wild parties."

Savvie shook her head, a little sad that she wouldn't be back to check in on Mrs. Smallwood. Before she'd left, she'd paid her rent through the end of the year and had left a potted gardenia for her landlord. It was her favorite flower. The woman had shed tears when Savvie had said she wouldn't be back.

Savvie had to admit, she'd miss the old lady. She'd always been smiling and singing softly to herself as she'd worked in her garden. Whenever she'd baked cookies, she'd brought some over to Savvie.

Mrs. Smallwood had invited her to Thanksgiving

dinner, claiming she'd made a feast and would just have to throw it away if Savvie didn't help her eat it.

She hadn't had a happy Thanksgiving since she was a little girl—before her parents had begun arguing. Before their divorce. Back when they could tolerate each other's company and showed some affection toward their only daughter.

"Do you have anything in storage you want to go get or send for?" Hunter asked.

She shook her head. "I donated everything to a woman's shelter. I only have the clothes on my back and some money stashed away. I left my apartment in Virginia knowing I wouldn't be back."

"It's hard starting over," Kyla said over her shoulder. "I came to West Yellowstone the same way. Just the clothes on my back. There's a great second-hand store with some things that might work for you here in town. You can order almost anything online. Or you can have one of the guys drive you up to Bozeman. Better yet, some of the guys' gals would love any excuse for a shopping trip." Kyla half-turned with a smile. "I'll pass. Shopping's not my thing. That and my ankles swell if I'm on my feet for too long a stretch."

The thought of a shopping trip with giggling females horrified Savvie. What did she have in common with normal women? Nothing. "I can make do with the consignment store. I'll need things I can wear to work."

"Have you thought about what you want to do for a job?" Kyla asked.

Savvie shook her head. "Not really. I have enough savings I could go a year or more before I have to find a full-time job." She shrugged. "I have no idea what to do or what I want to be when I grow up."

"Like you said, you have time to decide. You might want to join Lily and go to college for a degree."

Savvie shook her head. "No thanks. If I go back for something, it will be a trade. Maybe I'll learn how to weld, or operate a bulldozer or become a plumber."

"Sweetheart," Kyla said. "You don't have the butt crack to be a plumber. But if that's your dream, who am I to discourage a sister?"

Savvie laughed. "Thanks for your encouragement. It means a lot coming from you. You've figured out life outside the bubble of government employees or the military. Any advice?"

Kyla tilted her head to the side. "Yes, but I doubt you're ready to understand what I'm going to say."

"You have my full attention," Savvie said. "Fire away." Curious, she sat back.

"Since you have time, choose something that makes you happy. You need to give it a fair chance, but you don't have to commit the rest of your life to your choice. Later, you can change your mind and go in a different direction."

"Give my career choice a fair chance but don't be afraid to switch if my heart isn't in it." Savvie grinned. "Is that all?"

Kyla shook her head. "I think the most important thing to remember is to be open to exploring places and making new friends. And be open to falling in love." She squeezed Stone's hand. "I didn't believe in love. Thought it was a big bunch of hooey. Then it happened to me." She smiled, her face softening. "I've never been happier."

Stone lifted her hand and pressed a kiss to the backs of her knuckles. "Same. When you meet the right person, you don't want to waste another moment of your time apart from her."

"You want to get on with living the rest of your life with him." Kyla stared across the console at Stone, tears welling in her eyes. She swiped them away, laughing. "And when you do find the love of your life, you become one of those women you've always despised—a blubbering fool who cries at commercials and learns to crochet." Kyla shook her head. "Can you believe it? I'm learning how to crochet."

Savvie might not believe in love, but her friend did. The least she could do was be happy for her and keep her negativity to herself.

Even if love was real, who would want a woman who'd killed her stepfather and then had gone on to become an assassin?

She stole a glance at Hunter. He knew what she was and hadn't shrunk away. Then again, she wasn't asking him to date her or anything. He might be appalled at the idea.

Stone drove into the small tourist town of West Yellowstone and parked in front of a diner.

They all got out of the vehicle, moving slowly, working the kinks out of their bodies from sitting on a plane for the past four hours.

Kyla chose a table and chairs instead of a booth. "Can't squeeze in at this point."

The waitress brought coffee and took their orders.

Savvie stirred cream into her cup and poured in a couple of packets of sugar, her mind leaping ahead to the challenge of her future.

She stared around at the diner, watched the waitress take and deliver orders and interact with the customers with a smile.

It all seemed so bucolic and serene while there were people—women much like this waitress—being kidnapped and sold into the sex trade.

"Have you thought about what you want to do next?" Kyla asked.

"I could be a waitress," Savvie murmured softly.

"Yes, you could," Kyla said. "Just take your time. You might ask Stone's father, John Jacobs, if they need help maintaining the rooms and grounds of the lodge."

Savvie nodded absently.

So, she'd taken out one man in the business of capturing and selling women. What about the rest of the people in his organization? Why had she been sent to kill just one?

Marcus Caldwell's words returned to her. He'd called someone to report he had a woman who'd bring a good price. Marcus was just one of many in that organization trafficking souls.

"Are you okay?" Hunter had leaned close to whisper in her ear.

She shook her head. "No. Not really."

Kyla frowned. "You know, it's selfish of me to want food when the rest of you have obviously engaged in some serious hand-to-hand combat." Kyla laid her hand on Stone's arm. "Should we skip breakfast and get to the lodge? I can grab food there."

Savvie shook her head. "No. That's not necessary. I'm not sick, and my bruises aren't what's holding me back from moving on."

"No?" Kyla's brow wrinkled. "Then what's troubling you?"

No one had come to her rescue when her stepfather had nearly killed her mother. If she hadn't shot him with his own gun, he would have killed them both.

Savvie raised her gaze to meet Kyla's. "I'm troubled by some things Marcus Caldwell said when he thought I was passed out on the drugs he slipped into my drink and when he was trying to choke me to death."

Hunter touched her arm. "What did he say?"

"He said, *Got a blonde. You should get a good price for this bitch along with the others*." She turned to look into Hunter's eyes.

His brow furrowed. "...the others."

She nodded. "And when he had his hands around my throat, he said, *My brother doesn't like it when the goods are bruised and damaged*."

Hunter's lips thinned into a tight line. "The bastard deserved to die."

Savvie nodded. "Yes, but he's not the only one involved in the human trafficking business."

Stone's eyes narrowed. "The brother is in on it, and more victims are being held somewhere."

Savvie turned to Kyla.

The pregnant, former assassin held her gaze. "Why target only Marcus and not the rest of the trafficking ring?" Her brow dipped low. "I get the feeling someone in the Caldwell family has some strings to pull. Your handler gave you enough background on Marcus to get your buy-in to target him, but not anyone else."

"Yeah." Savvie's gut knotted. "In which case, I was played."

"The question is, by whom?" Kyla said. "And it could be more than one person."

"I need a computer," Savvie said, "and access to the internet. More specifically, the dark web."

"They followed you until we ditched our cell phones," Stone pointed out. "They have resources."

Savvie's lips curled back. "I have some resources of my own. I just need a computer and access."

"I think we can help you with that," Stone said. "Swede, our tech support wizard, will know what to do."

"If they have other victims being held captive, we need to move on this before they leave the country." Kyla tossed down her napkin. "That's it. I can get something to eat at the lodge. Let's go."

The waitress approached as they all stood.

"Sorry, I just remembered I left the iron on," Kyla said and sailed out of the diner.

Savvie chuckled and followed her lead. She'd worked solo for so long, it felt good to have people to help.

She just hoped that her role in targeting Marcus Caldwell didn't bring the wrath of the Caldwell mafia to West Yellowstone. She would never forgive herself if anything happened to Kyla and her baby.

CHAPTER 6

A FEW MINUTES LATER, the foursome entered the Grand Yellowstone Lodge and was greeted by the other two members of the Brotherhood Protectors who lived in West Yellowstone, along with the lodge's owner.

Stone made the introductions, nodding first to Savvie. "This is Savvie Sanders, Kyla's friend." He tipped his head toward the older man. "Savvie, my father, John Jacobs, owner of the lodge." He nodded toward the tallest man on the team. "Benjamin Yates, Navy SEAL."

Yates held out his hand. "You can call me Bubba," he said in a soft southern drawl.

Stone waved toward a shorter, wiry man. "And that's Morris Cleveland, our token Air Force para jumper."

The man held out his hand to Savvie. "Moe. Nice to meet you."

"Our other two team members, Carter Manning and Dax Young, are in Wyoming on assignment," Yates said.

John Jacobs smiled at Savvie. "Cookie has breakfast ready if you'd like to follow me to the dining room."

"If it's okay with you," Stone addressed his father, "we'd like to eat in the barn."

Savvie's brow twisted. "The barn?" she whispered to Hunter.

He chuckled. "The loft has been converted into our war room."

"I'll help Cookie load breakfast onto trays and bring it over along with coffee and juice," John offered.

"Thanks, Dad." Stone waved toward a door at the other end of the large lobby. "If you'll follow me, I'll take you to our command station."

Stone led the way out of the lodge and down a stone path to the barn. Once inside, they climbed a modern staircase up to the enclosed loft.

The space had been converted into a modern office space with a long conference table, storage rooms and cabinets, and computer stations with an array of monitors.

Kyla took a seat at one of the stations. "Welcome to my office," she said with a smile. "I traded field duty for a desk job, providing tech support to the team. Anything they need, from data mining to communications resources, I assist with, working closely with our computer genius, Swede. He's based out of the main headquarters in Eagle Rock, Montana, north of here."

Stone stepped up behind Kyla. "I think it would benefit us to debrief the big boss, Hank Patterson, on what happened in Miami."

"On it." Kyla ran her fingers over the keyboard.

Moments later, a huge screen lit up over one end of the conference table, and a man's face appeared.

"I'm Hank," the man nodded. "You must be Savvie Sanders."

Savvie nodded. "Yes, sir."

"You want to give me the sitrep on what happened in Miami?"

"Yes, sir." In an emotionless voice, Savvie gave Hunter's boss an abbreviated rundown of the events from the previous night. "I allowed myself to be lured to Marcus Caldwell's penthouse suite in the Setai Hotel, where he assumed he'd drugged me. When he placed a call to someone handling the movement of kidnap victims, I confronted him. There was a struggle, and I stabbed him in the jugular vein. He died."

Hunter marveled at Savvie's calm, collected version of a near-death experience.

"Caldwell's transfer team arrived before I could leave the penthouse. Their attempt to capture me was unsuccessful. I made it out of the hotel and contacted Kyla for assistance. Then I laid low until your team arrived. They can better describe our exit from Miami." She turned to Hunter.

Hunter's lips quirked as he described the blocked roads, the attack on the hotel path and their use of the wave runner to get off the island. "They knew where we were and rammed our rental vehicle in downtown Miami. We tossed our cell phones before we headed for the airport and made it back without further issues."

"Good call on the cell phones."

"I lost the burner phone I used to text Kyla in my fight with Marcus and his thugs," Savvie said. "I'd deleted the texts after I'd sent them, but I'm worried they'll find the phone and trace it back to Kyla, here in West Yellowstone."

"Stone?" Hank said.

"We'll tighten security. If we have any troubles, I'm bringing Kyla to your ranch."

"Like hell you are," Kyla interjected.

Stone laid a hand on her shoulder. "We can't risk your safety; you're too far along to protect yourself adequately."

She lifted her chin. "Says who?"

Stone kissed the top of her head. "You're the biggest—scratch that—baddest badass I've ever known. I'm sure you can take on anyone and come out the winner. But why risk it when you're eight months pregnant? Our baby needs to cook another four weeks to be on the safe side."

Kyla's lips twisted into a crooked frown. "It's hard being sidelined."

"…when you've been the quarterback on a team of one," Savvie finished. "Stone's right. Your baby needs you to protect him at all costs. If that means going someplace with tighter security, that's what you need to do." Savvie gave Kyla a weak smile. "I'm sorry if I've brought my problems to you. It might be better if I fly back to Miami. I shouldn't have left in the first place."

"You couldn't stay," Kyla said. "If the Caldwells didn't find you, you might've been found by the Miami police. From what we saw, they're treating Marcus's death as a homicide, and anyone who saw you leaving the bar with him would identify you as the killer."

"You killed him out of self-defense," Hunter reminded her.

"Doesn't matter," Savvie shook her head. "I can't go to the police and tell them that's what happened. I can't go to the police, period."

"She's right," Kyla said. "We were trained to avoid the police. As assassins, we perform our missions and disappear. We couldn't risk being caught. We're not even supposed to exist."

"The problem is that people saw Savvie leave the bar with Marcus Caldwell," Stone reminded them.

"And the guys who attacked her in his penthouse suite got a good look at her."

"Those men in his suite won't talk with the police," Savvie said. "They probably left before the police arrived and had someone tip off the hotel management to go check on Marcus. When they found Marcus, they saw the stab wound in his throat. It all looked like a murder occurred."

"And the bleach-blonde with whom he left the bar is the suspect they'll be looking for," Hunter concluded.

"What's bothering me most," Savvie said, "was that I was instructed to pose as a lighter-haired blonde, just as the other victims they'd already acquired. I got away. They did not."

Hunter's lips pressed together. "Who's looking for them?"

"I was lucky. I had a friend who sent people to save me." Savvie's gaze took in Kyla and Stone before stopping on Hunter. "Who will save them?" After a pause, she said, "Nobody."

HUNTER'S GUT TIGHTENED, an image from long ago of his car sinking beneath the surface of icy water coming back to haunt him. "It might already be too late," he said softly.

"What if it's not?" Savvie turned back to Hank. "What if we find them before they're sold?" She stared into the eyes of the man on the giant screen. "Hank, what's the name of your organization?"

"Brotherhood Protectors," he answered.

"What is your mission?" she demanded.

His chin rose. "To utilize our training and skills to protect, rescue or extract people in dangerous situations."

"What do you charge for your services?" Savvie asked.

"Whatever an individual can afford to pay." His lips quirked on the corners.

Hunter knew Hank hadn't turned away anyone who couldn't pay. He and his wife, Sadie, funded the organization out of their own pockets when necessary.

"I have money in a Swiss account," Savvie squared her shoulders. "I'll give it all to you if you help me save the others."

A petite, golden-haired blonde appeared behind Hank and laid a hand on his shoulder. "Keep your money," she said. "We'll help."

Hank covered her hand with his and smiled up at the woman adoringly. "I was just about to say that." He turned back to Savvie. "As my wife, Sadie, confirmed, we'll help."

A big, white-blond-haired Viking of a man rolled into view on an office chair. "Damn right, we will." He rolled back out of view.

Hank chuckled. "That's Swede. He's already

clicking through the internet, looking for information on the Caldwells."

"I'd like to get access to the internet, as well. I have some sources who might help." Savvie held up a hand. "I know how to redirect signals to keep others from tracing back to your IP address."

Swede rolled back in view with a grin. "I like the language you speak. We can get you set up where you can go just about anywhere on the web, and no one can find their way back to you."

"Perfect." She met his gaze with a direct one of her own. "How soon?"

Swede grinned. "Kyla has all the accesses needed. I can work with her to set you up on one of the Yellowstone computers. I'll need to isolate you so that if someone does get to your unit, they can't hack into the others. Give me a couple of hours."

John Jacobs and another man with a shock of white hair and bright blue eyes stepped into the war room, carrying trays laden with covered platters, a stack of plates, silverware, a carafe of orange juice and a pot of steaming coffee. As they set the trays on the conference table, the fragrant scent of coffee, bacon and toast filled the air.

Kyla groaned. "I could eat shoe leather I'm so hungry."

"Thankfully, you won't have to resort to sole food." John Jacobs set his tray on the conference table and chuckled softly at his own pun. He draped his arm atop the older man's shoulder. "This is perhaps the most important man in this outfit." He turned to smile at the older man. "This is Cookie, the best chef in the county."

The older man shrugged. "I don't know about best, but I know how to feed people."

John grinned. "That, he does. He fed an entire ship full of sailors when he was in the Navy. You should eat while the food is hot."

"You don't have to tell me twice." Kyla left her keyboard and took a seat at the conference table. "This baby is giving me hell this morning. It doesn't like it when my stomach is grumbling." She took the cover off one of the platters and inhaled deeply over a pile of bacon and sausage patties.

"Savvie," Hank said, "we'll get onto this and let you know what we find."

"Thank you." Savvie nodded, glad others were helping. "I'll look from my end as soon as I get my hands on a computer."

"While you're waiting for access to the computer and internet, you should check out West Yellowstone." Hank grinned. "Have you ever been to Yellowstone National Park?"

Savvie shook her head. "No."

"If you stay around for long, make sure you get over there," Hank said.

"Will do." Savvie gave the man a brief smile. "Thank you—and thank your wife for her support."

Hank's face lost all traces of his smile. "We're every bit as dedicated to freeing those women as you. But it might take time."

Hunter shook his head. "Time is something they might not have."

"Understood." Hank's lips pressed into a tight line. "We'll work as quickly as possible to find those women."

"As will we," Kyla said as she lifted a slice of toast in her hand. "At the same time, we'll try to find out who was behind getting the organization to target Marcus Caldwell and not the rest of his family and the human trafficking ring."

"Thank you," Savvie said. "I'm used to working on my own. It's nice to know I'll have help."

"It's what we do." Hank lifted his chin. "You know where to find us. Out here."

The screen went black.

Savvie turned to Hunter. "Thank you for getting me this far. I couldn't have done it without you, Stone and Kyla."

"I can't help you search the internet," Hunter said, "but when you discover where they're holding the other victims, I'm all in for the extraction."

Savvie touched his arm. "You've done a lot."

"And we have so much more to do. The thought of others being held in preparation for a sale…" He swallowed hard to clear his throat. When he'd been too late to save a young woman so long ago, he'd sworn he wouldn't let that happen again. He prayed they could find those souls before they were dispersed to their new owners and into a life so miserable he wouldn't wish it on his worst enemy.

"Sit," Kyla urged Savvie. "I'd apologize for diving into the food, but if I don't eat on time, my body reminds me what morning sickness is all about."

Hunter held a chair for Savvie.

She glanced toward the computers.

"I'll get back on it as soon as my food settles," Kyla said. "I guarantee Swede is tapping every source he has while we eat."

Savvie took the seat Hunter offered.

He sat beside her and handed her the platter of scrambled eggs.

They ate in silence, Hunter consuming protein in the form of eggs and sausage, fueling his body for whatever task might come next.

Savvie picked at her food, her brow knitted. When she finally pushed her plate away, she sighed. "I should've stayed in Miami."

"The way things were going, Caldwell's people would've caught up with you," Hunter said.

"If not them, the police would've found you and jailed you for the murder of a member of one of the wealthiest families in Florida," Stone said.

"Stone's right." Kyla lifted her toast in salute. "And what good would you have done from a jail cell?"

"If the Caldwells have that broad of a reach, you

wouldn't have been safe in a jail," Hunter said. "They wouldn't want you ratting out their money-making operation, even though they could probably buy their way out of any investigation."

Savvie's lips twisted. "I know all that, but how can I help the others when I'm more than halfway across the country?"

"We find where they're keeping them and send the feds in," Stone said.

Kyla snorted. "I wouldn't doubt it if someone with the feds was paid to put the hit on Marcus alone. Plus, the person paying had to be someone inside the trafficking ring getting a little power hungry."

"Why do you say that?" Stone asked.

"Why else target Marcus?" Kyla waved her hand. "They obviously wanted him out of the way without shutting down their operation. One less cut of the profits."

"Makes sense," Savvie murmured. "We should look at other members of the family and those in charge of acquisitions and sales."

Kyla tossed down her napkin and pushed back from the table. "After a quick trip to the bathroom, I'll get to it. Swede and I will also work on getting you up and running."

"In the meantime," Stone said, "Hunter can take you down to the lobby. My father will have a room for you. After being chased around Miami and a midnight excursion in the ocean, I'm sure you'd both like to shower."

Savvie stood, her cheeks flushing a pretty shade of pink. "I was limited on what I could bring in my backpack. Are there laundry facilities available?"

Hunter nodded. "Yes, they're located near the kitchen. I can show you where they are. In the meantime, I can loan you a T-shirt and sweatpants until we can get you to a store for clothes that better suit you."

She gave him a crooked smile. "Thanks."

"I also have some things that will work for you," Kyla said. "Lord knows they don't fit me in my condition. If you can make do with Hunter's stuff for now, I'll collect some things when I return to the lodge."

"Thank you," Savvie said. "As soon as I can arrange alternative lodging and clothing, I can be out of your hair. I don't want to be a burden on anyone."

Kyla pushed to her feet and crossed to where Savvie stood. "You don't have to make any quick decisions. You can stay as long as you want or need." She pulled her into her arms. "I'm glad you made it out alive. Get some rest."

Savvie hugged her friend. "Thank you, Kyla." She turned to the others in the room. "And thanks to the Brotherhood Protectors for coming to my rescue."

Hunter dipped his head. "If you're ready, we can find your room. I don't know about you, but that dried saltwater is starting to chafe against my skin."

Savvie grinned. "Ditto. I could use a shower, as well."

He led the way down the steps, out of the barn and back to the lodge.

John Jacobs stood behind the front desk, talking to a guest.

"Thank you for the recommendations, Mr. Jacobs," an older woman said. "My husband and I can't wait to visit the park. It's been on our bucket list for years. This is our first time to visit Montana and Wyoming, but I hope it won't be our last." She left with the map and brochure the lodge owner had been using to point out the highlights of the area.

When Mr. Jacobs turned his attention to Hunter and Savvie, he smiled. "Oh, good. I have a key for Ms. Sanders." He pulled a key out of a drawer and handed it to Savvie. "In case trouble followed you all the way out to Montana, it helps to have someone close who has your back. You'll be in the room next to Hunter. I assume he'll be your protector while you're here."

Savvie cocked an eyebrow toward Hunter. "My protector?"

Hunter nodded. "That's usually how it works with the team. If a friend, acquaintance or client needs protection or just to have someone nearby who has his or her back, that's where we come in. Not that anyone has been officially assigned to you," he assured her. "Not yet, anyway. If Stone or Hank decide you need that added layer of coverage..." he raised his hand, "I'm your man. After springing you from Miami, I feel like I have a vested interest in your well-being."

Savvie's lips pressed together. "I've worked on my own for years. I like to think I can take care of myself." Her lips quirked upward. "But it's nice to know I don't have to do this alone. Thanks."

Hunter's chest swelled. It had to have taken a lot for Savvie to admit she liked having a little help.

He was glad Mr. Jacobs had made the logical leap that Hunter would be Savvie's protector and had taken it upon himself to assign her the room next to Hunter's. If he hadn't, Hunter would have asked him to move her closer.

After being chased through Miami and their opposition showing up at every corner, Hunter would be surprised if the Caldwell mafia didn't follow Savvie out to Montana. "I'll show her to the room," he said.

Mr. Jacobs nodded. "Thanks. I have some things to check on." He tipped his head toward Savvie. "I left a variety of toiletries in the bathroom, figuring you might not have had time to pack your own."

"Thank you." Savvie smiled at the man. "Let me know what I owe you for them and the room."

"Hank has you covered," Mr. Jacobs said. "If you need anything else, don't hesitate to ask."

Hunter led the way across the open lobby with its

massive fireplace and comfortable seating and climbed a staircase to the second floor.

"The lodge is beautiful," Savvie commented as she looked out over the lobby below.

"Apparently, when Mr. Jacobs bought it, it was run down and needed a full remodel. He's done a lot of the overhaul himself." Hunter cupped her elbow and steered her down a hallway. "He said it had good bones and hated seeing it deteriorate."

Hunter appreciated the older Jacobs' attention to detail. He'd done his best to restore the original wood accents while adding sleek modern updates that blended old and new seamlessly.

Savvie ran her hand over the smooth wooden railing. "He's done a lovely job."

"There are still rooms that need work, but he gets to them when he can. We help when we have downtime. It's nice to work with your hands and see the results."

"Building versus killing?" Savvie sighed. "I can understand the appeal. I had similar thoughts in mind with my retirement from the organization."

"Oh yeah?" Hunter stared down at her. "Have you ever worked in construction?"

She laughed. "No, but I love watching the do-it-yourself shows that renovate old houses. I imagined doing one myself someday." Savvie shrugged. "They make it look easy."

Hunter grinned. "Some tasks can be fairly easy. Others…not so much." He stopped in front of a door.

Savvie looked up at him, her gray-blue eyes searching his. "You've worked in construction?"

He lifted a shoulder and let it fall. "As a junior and senior in high school, I worked summers helping my uncle flip houses."

"Oh, wow," her eyes widened. "Then you have skills."

He laughed aloud. "Most people would be more impressed at my range and accuracy as a sniper with Delta Force." He shook his head. "Nothing like someone in the same line of business to bring you back to the real world."

Savvie grinned, the first full smile of joy he'd seen that wasn't just a polite acknowledgment. It transformed her face from the serious beauty with small lines around her eyes to a younger, more carefree woman who didn't have years of experience as an assassin.

Hunter could almost imagine her before being recruited. Before she'd become a killer. At that moment, standing in the hallway, he wanted to kiss those pretty, happy lips.

As if drawn to her like a moth to a flame, he leaned closer.

The smile slipped from her face. Her gaze slid from his eyes to his mouth, and her chin tipped upward.

So close.

A door opened down the hallway, and the sound of voices made Hunter and Savvie's heads come up.

He stepped back at the same time as she did.

"Uh…" He dragged his mind back to the task at hand. "This is your room." He shoved the key into the lock, twisted it and pushed the door open. "I'm in the room next door." He tipped his head to the right. "If you need anything, you know where I am. Or you can just yell." He winked. "I'll hear you."

He handed her the key.

When their hands touched, an electric shock blasted through his system.

Her eyes flared for a moment, and then she lowered her lids. "Thanks for everything," she murmured and dove through the door, closing it between them.

For a long moment, Hunter stood, staring at the wood-paneled door, wishing he'd taken that kiss but knowing it would likely have been too much, too soon for Savvie.

He forced himself to enter his room.

Something about this woman had him thinking dangerous thoughts.

Thoughts about getting involved with a woman.

Chest-tightening fear raced through his body. He knew it, recognized it and had spent the better part of his adult life fighting its crippling effects.

The fact that she was an assassin didn't faze him

in the least. He'd been a sniper. Many times, he'd dropped a specific target. Wasn't that the same thing? He wasn't afraid of her or the skills she'd honed over the years in the trade.

What he was afraid of was caring for her, like he'd cared for others and lost them despite his attempts to save them.

Starting with Sarah.

Hunter strode into the bathroom, stripped out of his clothes and dropped them into the laundry basket. When he turned on the shower faucet, he left the temperature on cold, needing the wake-up call to reality. He'd help Savvie as much as he could, but he had to leave his heart out of it.

She was starting over, free of her former career, open to starting a new life. If she let someone close, it needed to be someone who wasn't afraid. Someone who could commit his heart and soul to her.

That someone wasn't him.

CHAPTER 7

WHEN SAVVIE HAD DARTED into her room and closed the door between her and Hunter, she'd stood for a long moment, holding her breath, listening for the sounds of his footsteps walking away.

He hadn't moved for long enough that she'd had to draw another breath. Then the footsteps tapped softly, a door opened and closed, and silence reigned.

Savvie inhaled a deep breath and let it out slowly, willing her pulse to slow.

For a moment in the hallway, she'd thought Hunter was going to kiss her. He'd leaned toward her, his gaze on her lips, his face lowering to hers.

She pressed a hand to her chest to ease the ache that had settled in her heart. Sweet Jesus, she'd wanted him to kiss her.

And what would that have accomplished?

Not a damned thing.

Starting something with Hunter was a one-way ticket to heartbreak. Even if the Caldwell mafia wasn't after her, any one of the family or allies of her previous hits could discover her identity and come after her.

She wasn't concerned for her own safety, but she was concerned for the safety of those around her. Anyone she might care about would become a target to get to her. She couldn't endanger Hunter, Kyla or anyone else in West Yellowstone by just being there.

She strode through the room, pulling the T-shirt over her head. In the bathroom, she kicked off her shoes, dropped her jeans and stepped free of them. Standing in her bra and panties, she turned on the water in the shower and let it warm. When it was just right, she unhooked her bra, shucked her panties and stepped beneath the spray.

As water ran over her head and shoulders, she raised her face to the spray in an attempt to wash the Delta Force sniper from her mind.

It didn't work.

The warm water caressed her skin and ran in rivulets over her chest and down her torso. She could imagine what it would feel like to have Hunter's fingers tracing the droplets down the length of her throat, over her collarbone and the swell of her breasts to slip off the tips of her nipples.

Heat coiled at her core, spreading through her

body, making her sex throb with a need she hadn't experienced in a long time.

A laugh caught in her throat at the idea of need. Hadn't Hunter said that if she needed anything, all she had to do was yell? What would he do if she told him she needed him for sex?

Hell, he was a guy. He might be okay with satisfying her *need*. What about his needs?

Was Hunter the kind of guy who'd expect more after sex? Would he want to make a big deal out of a one-night stand?

If he expected more, could she face him in a room full of his friends, knowing sex was all she could give him?

No. Sex wasn't in the cards for her and Hunter. She was already in debt to these people for saving her life and getting her out of Miami before whoever was after her got to her first.

She poured shampoo into her hand and scrubbed the salt and sand from her hair. Then she scrubbed her body, her hands sliding over her breasts and down to the juncture of her thighs.

She didn't need a man to satisfy her needs. Years alone had taught her she was responsible for her own orgasms.

Savvie parted her folds and touched the tip of her finger to her clit, swirling it around and around.

"You don't need a man to do this," she coached herself softly. Closing her eyes, she imagined a man touching her there, going down on her and flicking her with the tip of his tongue. She tapped herself, swirled and flicked.

She sucked in a breath and held it, willing the rush of sensations to take control and send her over the edge as it had so many times in the past.

Her mind drifted to the man in the room next door.

He was probably naked. Like her.

Standing in the shower. Like her.

Was he touching himself?

Her finger moved faster.

Had he been turned on by a near-kiss?

If she let him into her room, would he be a good lover? Would he be gentle? Or would he be so consumed by passion that he'd go hard and fast?

Savvie's pulse sped, and her breathing grew ragged. "Hard and fast, please." She alternated between thrusting her fingers into her channel and teasing her clit until an explosion rocked through her, sending a wave of release throughout her body.

By the time the rush faded, the water had grown cool.

Savvie turned off the shower, wrapped a fluffy white towel around her body and stepped out onto the mat.

Her heart still pounding, she stood for a moment, congratulating herself on her own ability to satisfy her needs sans a male partner.

The sudden knock on the door to her room sent her heartbeat back into overdrive.

She hurried across to answer, clutching the towel around her.

With her hand on the doorknob, she called out, "Who's there?"

"Me," Hunter's deep tone answered.

Holy hell. She glanced at the bathroom door she'd left open throughout her shower. Had she called his name aloud?

Heat burned up her neck into her cheeks. "Just a minute." Her gaze swept the room, looking for something she could throw on. Oh yeah, she didn't have any clean clothes, and she sure as hell wasn't going to climb back into what she'd just taken off.

"Hey," his muffled voice came through the wood paneling, "I have a T-shirt and sweats for you. I can leave them on the floor outside."

"No, that's okay." She pulled open the door wide enough for him to pass the items through. And wide enough, she could see him on the other side, wearing nothing but a pair of jeans, zipped but not buttoned.

Savvie struggled to breathe. As she took the shirt and sweats from his hands, her fingers touched his and set her blood burning through her veins, headed straight south to her still-throbbing core.

His brow wrinkled. "Are you all right?"

"Y-yes," she stuttered. "Of course. Why do you ask?"

"Your cheeks are flushed. Are you sure you're not coming down with something?" He reached out to touch his palm to her forehead and then her cheek.

Savvie froze. She couldn't have moved from where she stood if she'd tried.

Instead, she leaned her face into his open hand. "I'm fine," she said, unable to get enough air past her vocal cords to be any louder than a whisper.

His frown deepened. "You're a little warm."

She wasn't just warm. She was hot.

With nothing but a towel between her skin and his naked chest, she was getting hotter. All she had to do was loosen her hold on the towel...

He stared into her eyes for a long moment, his gaze slipping lower to her mouth, his head dipping downward.

All she had to do was rise an inch or two, and their lips would meet.

A shiver of awareness rippled across her skin.

Hunter's hand dropped to his side. "You must be cold. When you're dressed and ready, we can go down together. I can show you around the grounds if you'd like."

She nodded and managed to say, "I'd like that." *And a whole lot more.* "I won't be long."

He stepped back.

She closed the door and could have kicked herself for not closing the distance between their lips. The anticipation of kissing the man was heady. Would the reality be as titillating?

She'd never know because it would be a mistake. Jesus. How many times did she have to remind herself?

Savvie hurried to the bathroom, towel-dried her hair, found a new brush Mr. Jacobs had left for her and worked through the tangles from the wild ride among the ocean waves, holding tightly around Hunter's middle.

Having seen his bare abs, she had a whole new appreciation for that waist she'd clung to for the long ride around Miami Beach.

Once she had her damp hair smoothed back from her forehead and lying straight down around her shoulders, she pulled Hunter's T-shirt over her head. It hung down to the middle of her thighs. Savvie nixed the idea of wearing it as a dress just yet. She had no panties to wear beneath it, and she wasn't comfortable parading around the lodge among other guests with nothing underneath.

She pulled on the sweatpants Hunter had delivered with the shirt and cinched the drawstring tightly to keep them snuggly around her hips.

Her lady parts tingled at the thought that Hunter had worn these pants. Did he go commando in them?

"Get a grip, Savvie," she chided herself.

She had gone a long time without getting laid. Now wasn't the time to remedy that situation.

Finding the other victims of the human trafficking ring was more important than scratching her itch.

Even though they were still a little damp with saltwater, Savvie pulled on her tennis shoes and tied the laces.

With no makeup, her hair pulled back from her face, and wearing clothes that were too big for her, she looked like a homeless street urchin.

That was a good thing.

Hunter wouldn't find her the least bit attractive.

As she stood at the door, she hesitated. At the last minute, she pulled the T-shirt up and knotted one side at her waist. She might look like a street urchin, but maybe a slightly hipper street urchin.

She yanked open the door and stepped out, nearly plowing into the man standing there.

Hunter chuckled, his hands coming up to grab her arms to steady her. "In a hurry? I wasn't going to leave without you."

The heat generated from where his hands curled around her bare arms burned through her veins and into her cheeks.

"Sorry. I took too long and didn't want to keep you waiting."

"You didn't. I just got here and was about to knock—"

"—when I plowed into you like a klutz. Silly me." She bit down on her tongue to keep from uttering more inane words. Now, she was a street urchin who couldn't make adult conversation. Where was the badass assassin, unafraid of anything and anyone? She squared her shoulders. "Please, show me the grounds, and then, maybe, Kyla and Swede will have word on the other victims or have a computer I can use to help find them."

The sooner they found the others, the sooner they could free them. Then she could disappear with a clear conscience and leave these people to continue their good work helping others. They'd be safer without her.

Hunter led her down the staircase to the lobby and into a room filled with tables and chairs.

"This is the dining room." He lifted his chin toward a long table with a dozen chairs around it. "We usually eat at the big table for our meals and help clean up afterward. Cookie's a helluva chef and manages to cook for the staff as well as the guests. We pitch in when we can."

"That could be a lot of meal prep for one man," Savvie commented. "Would it help if we cooked our own meals?"

Hunter laughed. "Cookie is a retired Navy cook. He fed every sailor on board the ships he sailed with. After the Navy, he was recruited by the White House to cook State dinners. Apparently, he got tired of big-city life and came to work with Mr. Jacobs when he needed a chef for the lodge. Said it was like a vacation."

"The lodge is lucky to have him." Savvie was impressed. "I can imagine he has a great repertoire of recipes after working at the White House."

"He does. If we don't know what the dish is, we don't ask until after we've eaten. Everything he makes tastes amazing."

"The breakfast was very good," Savvie said.

Hunter led the way through the dining room into the kitchen, where the man they'd been discussing was up to his elbows in flour, kneading a huge ball of dough.

"Hey, Cookie." Hunter nodded to the retired Navy chef. "Just giving Savvie a tour of the lodge and grounds."

Cookie lifted his chin without taking his hands off the dough. "Making tonight's dinner rolls." He leaned his head toward the counter. "Made some chocolate chip cookies this morning. Take some with you."

Hunter crossed to the indicated counter and took the top off a clear glass jar filled to the rim with cookies. He took out two of the treats and replaced the lid. "Thanks, Cookie. You make the best chocolate chip cookies."

"Damn right, I do," he said.

Handing one of the cookies to Savvie, Hunter passed through the kitchen to a door on the other side. He pushed the door open into a laundry room with a row of industrial washing machines, dryers and four regular washing machines.

"You can do your laundry here. They use the big machines for the lodge bedding and towels." He walked through to a door on the other side that led out to the far end of the lobby. "You don't have to go through the kitchen to get to the laundry room."

"Good to know," she said.

As they stepped out into the lobby, Kyla came through the back door and smiled when she spotted them. "There you are."

"Do you have a computer I can use?" Savvie asked.

"Soon," Kyla promised. "I've been working with Swede to download software and firewalls to keep hackers from tapping into our IP address. In fact, it's still downloading. I'm taking a break to find you something to wear other than Hunter's hand-me-downs." Kyla tipped her head. "Although, you wear them well. Whatever I find that might fit you, I'll leave at your door."

"Thank you," Savvie said.

Kyla switched her attention to Hunter. "You should take Savvie to the general store for other things she might need."

Savvie shook her head. "Until I can access my bank, I don't have any cash on me, and I don't dare use any of my credit cards. Not here."

Kyla nodded. "The lodge has an account at the general store. Just tell them to put it on that account. I'll have John call ahead to let them know you're coming."

"I'll pay him back," Savvie promised.

"I know," Kyla said. "Check back in an hour or two. We should have a computer ready for you."

"I assume you haven't found any leads on the whereabouts of the other victims Marcus mentioned," Savvie queried.

Kyla's lips pressed together. "I have my contacts checking around, and Swede put out feelers on the dark web. We hope we hear something soon."

"Yeah. Me, too." Savvie sighed. "I should've let them take me to the others. Then at least, I'd know where they were."

Kyla shook her head. "You dodged the drugs in your drink. I doubt they'd take you out of the hotel without hitting you with something even stronger."

"Then you'd be just like the other women. Too doped up to escape," Hunter said. "You did right to get out while you could. Drug-free, even at a distance, you have more of a chance of helping them than incapacitated with whatever they're using to keep their merchandise subdued."

"He's right," Kyla said. "We don't have to tell you that. You know it's true, so stop second-guessing yourself. I'll see you in a bit. I need to get you some clothes and get back to my terminal." Kyla hurried away pretty fast for a woman who was eight months pregnant.

"I don't think pregnancy has slowed her down in the least," Savvie said.

Hunter chuckled. "Not at all. Stone has to remind her to take it easy for the baby's sake." Hunter held the back door of the lobby open for Savvie.

As they stepped out onto the wide porch, Savvie took time to appreciate the view this time. The last time, she'd been in a hurry to get to the Brotherhood Protectors' office above the barn. Knowing she couldn't do much to help until she had access to the internet, she drank in the fresh mountain air and the scent of evergreens.

"This place is beautiful," she said.

"It gets busy with tourists in the summer as well as the winter," he commented. "People come to see Yellowstone National Park, but there's only so much lodging at the park. West Yellowstone is the nearest town of any size, so it's a hopping-off point for people to visit. It's also an angler's paradise with the rivers so close. The fishing is great."

"You know, I've never been fishing," Savvie said.

His eyes widened. "Never been fishing? Didn't your dad ever take you?"

Her jaw tightened. "I never knew my father."

Hunter stopped walking. "I'm sorry."

She shrugged. "I didn't miss what I didn't have. It was my mother and me for a long time."

"And then she remarried?"

"Married for the first time," Savvie corrected.

"And your stepfather never took you fishing?" Hunter asked gently.

Savvie shook her head. "I was fourteen when they married." She turned and walked toward the barn.

Hunter fell in step beside her. "And you weren't too happy about your mother's choice. Tell me to shut up if I'm getting too personal."

"It's okay," she said. Maybe if he knew about her past, he'd run the other way. She wouldn't have to worry that he might kiss her, and she might let him. "He was okay at first. Mom was happy and thought herself in love."

Hunter didn't comment. He walked slowly, letting her tell the story with as much or as little detail as she wanted.

"When the honeymoon phase wore off, his true self shone through. Things weren't going so well for him at his job. So, he came home angry most evenings. Sometimes, he stopped at his favorite bar for drinks first. Mom worked as a clerk at a grocery store. After being on her feet all day, she came home, cooked dinner and cleaned up after him."

Savvie remembered how tired she'd been and how she hadn't smiled as much as she had that first year with Ralph.

Savvie had helped by cooking some nights and picking up after her stepfather, who couldn't seem to carry an empty beer can from the end table beside his lounge chair to the trash can. Ever.

She'd cleaned up after him, not for him, but for her mother.

"The more dissatisfied he got with his job, the more he verbally abused my mother. Verbal abuse became physical abuse. I remember the first time he slapped her and the shock on her face. I was fifteen. I'd never seen a man slap a woman before. I was as stunned as my mother."

"No man has the right to hit a woman," Hunter said through gritted teeth.

"No man or woman has the right to physically or mentally abuse another." She snorted softly. "Says the assassin. I must be a hypocrite."

"You were following orders…doing your job."

"Murdering people." She stopped walking and turned to face Hunter. "By the time I was seventeen, my stepfather went past slapping to knocking my mother across the room. When I tried to stop him, he knocked me across the room as well."

Hunter's hands bunched into fists. "Why didn't you and your mother get out?"

"Mom refused to leave him." Savvie's lip curled up on one side. "When I was seventeen, I came home from my after-school job to find him punching my mother like a prizefighter. When she fell to the floor, he kicked her again and again. I yelled at him to stop. He didn't. When I jumped in front of him, he backhanded me so hard that he slammed me against the wall.

"My mother dragged herself up and told him to stop, but he went back to punching her. I walked into their bedroom, got the gun out of his nightstand and came back into the living room where he had my mother on the floor again, yelling at her and kicking her in the ribs."

Savvie paused, her gaze on the ground in front of her. She lifted her chin and met Hunter's glance. "I told him to stop. He didn't. So, I shot him."

"Oh, Savvie." Hunter reached out.

She backed away. "I only winged him in the arm. He turned toward me, rage making his face red and the veins on his forehead stick out." She'd never forget the pure evil in his face and eyes. She'd had nightmares for years with that face coming at her.

"He charged me like a bull. I shot him three more times. He didn't fall until he reached me. Then he dropped, taking me down with him. I hit my head against the wall. I must have blacked out for a moment. When I came to, I couldn't breathe." Savvie closed her eyes, reliving the panic she'd felt when she couldn't catch her breath all those years ago.

"His weight was crushing my lungs. I fought to get out from under him. It took everything I had to move him enough to pull free. By the time I got to my feet, I was covered in his blood. He didn't move. He was dead."

She looked back at the ground as if seeing her stepfather's lifeless body, the magnitude of what she'd done hitting her like a freight train.

"Your mother?" Hunter asked quietly.

"She was lying on the floor, staring at my stepfather. She could barely talk because she was in so much pain from the broken ribs he'd given her. I remember what she said." Savvie stared into Hunter's eyes, her brows pulled together in a frown.

He waited for her to continue.

She swallowed hard, her heart squeezing so tightly in her chest she couldn't breathe. "*He's dead, isn't he?* When I nodded, her face turned white, and her eyes got really big. Then she said, *What have you done?*"

CHAPTER 8

HUNTER TOOK Savvie's hands in a gentle grip. When she didn't pull free, he tugged lightly, bringing her close. Slowly, he wrapped his arms around her.

He didn't hold her tightly. If she wanted to be free, all she had to do was step back.

She didn't.

For a long moment, she stood, her body stiff, her breathing labored. "The last time I told anyone what happened was in front of a judge when I was held for the murder of my stepfather."

"Couldn't they see that you'd done it in self-defense?" He smoothed a hand down her back in a soothing, repetitive motion. "Didn't your mother tell the police what happened?"

Savvie snorted softly. "She told the police that I'd killed him." Her head moved side to side. "No. She screamed to them that I'd killed him. She continued to scream as they loaded her into the ambulance."

"Oh, Savvie." Hunter's fingers gripped her upper arms.

Savvie leaned back and glared up into his eyes. "Don't you dare feel sorry for me. You're the first person I've told what happened outside the court. I didn't tell you so that you could feel sorry for me." Though she'd leaned back, she didn't leave his embrace.

"Okay. I won't feel sorry for you." Hunter brushed a strand of her hair off her cheek. "But I want to understand what happened."

She allowed him to bring her close again. "I just told you. I killed my stepfather."

"Defending yourself and your mother against that bastard."

"Yeah, well, it didn't help that my mother called me a murderer."

"They took you into custody?"

Savvie nodded, the stiffness in her back easing slightly. "I was sent to a juvenile detention center because my mother was in no condition to care for me. I was in the detention center through most of my last year of high school. I finished by taking the GED."

"Smart."

She shrugged. "I couldn't have gone back to my school. Everyone thought of me as a cold-blooded murderer. Besides, I had to have my day in court. Because of the nature of the crime and the fact I was seventeen, they tried me as an adult."

"And they saw reason and let you walk away, free," Hunter concluded. "Otherwise, you wouldn't have been able to join a government para-military assassination team. You'd have been classified as high risk."

Her lips twisted. "After high school, I was going to join the Marines. They pulled me out at MEPS to interview for the organization. They'd studied my background. They asked me if I was given the same situation with my mother and stepfather, would I do it again?"

"What did you say?" Hunter held his breath.

"I said *without hesitation.*" Her fingers curled into the soft cotton T-shirt he wore.

He liked the way her fingernails scraped across his skin beneath the jersey. "It was him or you and your mother. You had to do it. Did your mother ever clear up her version of the event?"

Savvie leaned her forehead against his chest. "No. Ralph had kicked her so many times with his steel-toed boot she had internal injuries and bleeding. She spent the last days of her life in the hospital. They couldn't stop the bleeding. It turned into an infection. She wouldn't forgive me for killing her husband. My mother claimed she had nothing left to live for, so she died."

"Wow." Hunter couldn't believe a mother would

put that guilt on her child. Because she didn't want his pity, he didn't say he was sorry, though he was. He stood in silence for a long time, holding her.

Her stiffness faded until she melted into him and wrapped her arms around his waist.

"My mother didn't forgive me. That hurt. But I wouldn't have forgiven myself if I'd let that bastard continue to beat her. I should've killed him sooner. She might still be alive today."

"They recruited you to be an assassin. What made you accept?" he asked.

She looked up at him. "They promised me that the people I would target were bad. They gave me their dossiers prior to the missions. I did my own research as well. My hits were truly bad people who'd done terrible things to others. In a way, I was trying to save more people like my mother from being abused or murdered. The world is a better place without people like Marcus Caldwell."

She looked away. "But I only did a fraction of the job. There's more work to be done to shut down their operation and free the people they've captured."

With his thumb, Hunter turned her gaze back to him and stared down into her eyes, his heart swelling at the passion and conviction reflected in their gray-blue depths. "You're not manning this mission solo anymore. *We* will finish the job."

Her brow furrowed. "I worry that bringing your people in on this task will put them in danger."

"It's what we do," he said. "We chose to be a part of Brotherhood Protectors, knowing the job would be risky. We accepted that risk when we signed on. All of us are prior military. We've fought in wars and know what it means to run into a hot zone."

"But Kyla…" Savvie shook her head. "Her baby didn't sign up for danger. What if by helping me, we put her baby at risk?"

"The team will make sure Kyla and her baby are safe. You know her." He brushed his thumbs across Savvie's cheeks. "She won't back down. She's just as much a part of the team as the rest of us. When she commits to a task, she's like a pit bull with a bone. She'll sink her teeth in and won't let go until the mission is complete."

Savvie's lips twisted into a faint smile. "She was that way during our training. She was completely focused and one hundred percent badass."

Hunter smiled down at her. "Like you. Seeing you in action when we met up was impressive. And you managed to get away from a man choking you *and* his two thugs. That's badass in my books." He bent and brushed a kiss across her forehead.

The gesture sent a blast of heat all the way to his groin. If that little flutter of a kiss elicited that much of a reaction, he could only imagine what a full-on kiss would generate.

His gaze shifted to her lips, and he lowered his head.

The sound of an engine firing up broke through the trance he'd fallen into the moment he'd wrapped his arms around Savvie.

She blinked, stiffened and stepped away.

A tractor emerged from one of the storage buildings and rumbled toward them. The man driving it waved, bringing the machine to a halt beside them. He shifted into neutral, set the brake and climbed down.

"You must be the new girl," he said and held out his hand. "I'm Tinker, resident maintenance and handyman."

Hunter didn't know whether to curse the man or thank him for his untimely interruption. Had he not come out when he had, Hunter would have kissed Savvie. Not a brotherly brush of the lips across her forehead. He'd have claimed her mouth with all the passion roiling beneath his surface.

The woman had enough to worry about. She didn't need a relative stranger hitting on her.

She'd just opened up to him, spilling her guts about the event that had changed her life forever.

What a jerk to take advantage of her when she had to be overwhelmed with memories. Not to mention, she probably suffered from PTSD from the abuse she'd experienced at the hands of her stepfather. And then to be rejected by her dying mother...

He wanted to wrap her in his arms and keep her there, taking away all the pain and sadness.

Hell, she was a trained assassin, used to operating solo. She didn't need him to shield her from danger and probably wouldn't appreciate any attempt to do so.

If he wanted to help Savvie, he'd have to treat her as an equal, someone who could fight alongside him, not take a backseat to any threat.

Tinker shook Savvie's hand. "Hunter giving you the tour of the grounds?"

Savvie smiled at the man. "He is."

"Check out the last stall in the barn." Tinker tilted his head toward the structure. "Someone left a surprise there last night."

Hunter frowned. "Who left what?"

Tinker shrugged. "Guess you'll have to find out for yourself." He climbed up onto the tractor. "Got some mowing to do, or I'd show you myself." Tinker shifted the tractor into gear, and it lurched forward. Moments later, he disappeared around the side of the lodge.

"Tinker's a retired Marine. Spent his military service in the motor pool. He can fix anything. In fact, he's got an old Abrams tank behind the barn he's been working on since I've known him."

Savvie's eyes widened. "Seriously?"

Hunter nodded. "Not sure what he plans to do with it once he gets it running. It's a favorite with the children of the guests. They can climb all over it."

"Is everyone who works here prior military?" she asked.

Hunter grinned. "I guess so if you count your organization as a secret branch of the military. Kyla's the only one who didn't serve in one of the traditional branches of service."

"Mr. Jacobs?" she asked.

"Marine." Hunter turned toward the barn.

Savvie fell in step beside him.

He reached out a hand and captured hers.

She didn't resist.

They walked together the rest of the way, hand in hand.

Hunter liked the feel of her slender fingers resting in his palm. He admired the strength in her hand. When they reached the barn, he had to release his grip to open the door. He stood back, allowing her to enter first.

When they'd been in the barn earlier, they'd gone straight up to the war room in the loft.

This time, Hunter took the time to show Savvie around the lower level of the large structure.

He opened a door leading into a room to the right. "This is the tack room where we keep the saddles, bridles, brushes, medications and anything you might need for the few horses that reside here. You're more than welcome to ride any one of them. They're all well-trained and easy to handle." He glanced at Savvie. "Maybe I should ask first... Do you ride?"

Savvie shook her head. "Never have. I grew up in Atlanta. When I was eight, I asked for riding lessons for my birthday. Mom could barely afford to put food on the table. There was no way she could've afforded riding lessons."

Hunter tilted his head. "It's never too late to learn. I could teach you."

She smiled up at him. "I'd like that, but I don't think I'll be around long enough."

Hunter's chest tightened. He didn't want to think of Savvie moving on and leaving West Yellowstone. Against his better judgment and years of avoiding involvement, he couldn't squelch the desire to get to know her better. "The offer remains open. You should at least let me show you the basics. Then you can decide whether you want to learn more when you settle on a place to live." He hoped that place she settled on was right there in the small Montana town.

"You have a good point," she said.

He led the way out of the tack room and stopped in front of one of the stalls.

"This is Rusty." The sorrel gelding poked his head over the top of the gate and nuzzled Hunter's hand.

"Sorry, dude." He held up his empty hands for the horse to inspect. "No apple today."

Rusty tossed his head, clearly annoyed that

Hunter hadn't brought him the usual treat. He settled for a scratch behind the ears.

They moved to the next stall, where a palomino mare whinnied softly.

"Hey, Duchess." Hunter stroked the mare's nose. "Duchess is the grand dame of the trio. She has the most grace and sweetest temperament."

Savvie reached out and touched the mare's nose. "She's so soft."

The mare lifted her head, sniffed Savvie's hair and then lowered her head for more petting.

Savvie smiled. "She's beautiful."

Hunter leaned toward Savvie and whispered in a conspiratorial voice, "I think she knows it."

"As she should," Savvie said. "Isn't that right, Duchess?"

Duchess tossed her head in agreement.

Savvie chuckled.

The sound warmed Hunter's heart. He wanted her to make the sound more often. She probably hadn't had many occasions to laugh.

The next stall contained a bay gelding. "This is Frisco. He's younger than the other two and a little higher strung, but he usually settles down once you're in the saddle."

Frisco draped his head over the stall gate and nibbled at Savvie's hair.

"Dude," she said, "it may look like hay, but it's not."

Savvie pulled her hair behind her ears and looked around.

Hunter stood in the middle of the barn. "That's all the horses for now. Hank and Stone had originally planned to convert the entire barn into offices, but we all agreed we had enough room in the loft and would rather use the lower portion of the barn for its original purpose."

He waved to the other side of the barn, where a collection of machines lined the wall. "We have a collection of four-wheelers and snowmobiles we can use to get around in the mountains if we don't want to take the horses." He looked around. "So, that's the barn. And you know what's upstairs. The other large outbuilding is where the tractor and implements are stored and where Tinker works on anything that needs to be fixed. All his tools are stored there."

Savvie's gaze went to the last stall at the end of the barn. "Aren't you curious about the surprise Tinker mentioned?"

Hunter laughed. "I am. I was waiting for you to say something. Come on. Let's check it out."

They walked to the last stall.

Hunter looked over the gate and didn't see anything but wood shavings on the stall floor. "Hmm. I don't see anything." He opened the door and stepped inside.

Something moved in the corner to his left. He

pulled his cell phone out of his pocket, turned on the flashlight app and shined it into the corner.

A pair of eyes blinked at him, and a soft meow sounded in response to being blinded by the light.

Hunter approached slowly and squatted in front of an orange tabby cat curled up in the corner. "Hey, there. You're the cat I've seen hanging around."

The cat turned and licked at tiny little mouse-like creatures pressed against her belly.

"What is it?" Savvie asked from the gate.

"Come see," he invited and moved aside so Savvie could kneel next to him.

He shined the light onto the mama cat and her litter of kittens.

"Oh," Savvie sat back on her heels. "They're so tiny."

"She must have had them recently." Hunter studied the little ones. "I count five. What do you get?"

Savvie nodded. "Five. Two orange tabbies like their mama, two gray and whites and one calico."

"Eventually, we'll have to find homes for the kittens and catch mama to have her spayed. But for now, she's got a warm, dry place to keep them safe." Hunter pushed to his feet and backed out of the stall.

Savvie stood for a moment longer, a smile curling the corners of her lips. When she stepped through the gate, she gave him a wistful smile. "I never had a pet growing up."

"Not even a cat?"

Her lips twisted into a frown. "We lived in an apartment that didn't allow animals. When we moved into Ralph's house, he had a fenced backyard, perfect for a dog." She shook her head. "He refused to let us get a dog. A neighbor's dog strayed into his front yard once, tail wagging and eager to make a new friend. He kicked it so hard it cried all the way back to his home." Savvie's lips pressed together in a tight line.

"How a man treats animals says a lot about his character," Hunter noted.

"True." Savvie sighed. "After that, I didn't ask for a pet. He would have hurt it, too. I would never subject an animal to that kind of abuse."

"I grew up near a small town in the Hill Country of Texas," Hunter said. "We had a small farm, raised a few cows, rode horses and had a variety of pets. Of course, the usual cats and dogs. I had a miniature donkey that followed me around. She thought she was one of the dogs. We trained her to pull a little cart in the annual Fourth of July parade." He smiled. "I haven't thought about Annabel for a long time."

"You have brothers and sisters?" she asked.

He nodded. "Two sisters and one brother. I was number three of four. During the summer, we ran wild like feral cats. We'd leave the house first thing in the morning and didn't come back until dark. Our friends would come from town, and we'd ride horses, go fishing, swim in the creek and camp out under the stars."

"Sounds like you had an idyllic childhood," Savvie said. "Why didn't you stay in your small town? What made you join the Army?"

Hunter's smile faded, and his gaze moved from Savvie to the far corner of the barn. "Things happened. I couldn't stay." He'd gotten out as soon as he'd graduated high school and hadn't gone back since. Not even to visit his family.

"Hunter?" Savvie frowned up at him. "What happened?"

He stood silent, unhappy memories pushing out the good ones.

"It's okay. You don't have to tell me." Savvie touched his arm. "Although, what could be worse than shooting your stepfather?"

He gave a short bark of laughter that held no joy. "What could be worse than killing a man who deserved to die?" He steeled himself for the rush of guilt and regrets that never failed to overwhelm him when he thought back to that fateful day. "What's worse is killing your high school sweetheart."

CHAPTER 9

OF ALL THINGS Hunter could have said, Savvie hadn't expected that.

"You killed your high school sweetheart?" She shook her head. "Surely, it was an accident."

Hunter ran a hand through his hair. "I was young, invincible and stupid. Unfortunately, I took Sarah along for my ride of stupidity."

"Okay," Savvie said, "that's clear as mud." She took his hand and walked him to the stairs leading up to the war room and sat, pulling him down beside her. "Care to enlighten me?" she urged softly.

He shook his head. "Not really."

"Then we'll just sit here. I have nowhere else I have to be." Her thoughts ran with what little he'd said. How could he have killed his high school sweetheart?

Had he been in a jealous rage? She looked at his

face. The shadows beneath his eyes made him appear sad, even haunted.

Savvie hadn't known Hunter long, but she knew this man wasn't her stepfather. He would never hurt a woman in a fit of rage or anything else.

Hunter leaned forward and buried his face in his hands. For a long moment, he remained unmoving.

Savvie figured he wasn't going to tell her what had happened. And she wasn't going to press for the details. She understood the effects of trauma, having lived through her own version. If he didn't want to talk about it, she wasn't going to push him.

Not knowing how to comfort him, she laid her hand on his back. She didn't move it up and down, just let it lay there on his taut muscles. She hoped that the warmth of her hand let him know she was there for him.

Hunter sat up straight and scrubbed a hand down his face. "I was eighteen, a senior in high school, planning on going to college the next fall. Sarah and I had applied to the same university. We had our lives mapped out. We had a plan." He stared straight ahead as if seeing his past replaying like a silent movie.

"It was February, and we'd had a cold snap. It had started to rain, but it was Friday night. I refused to let a little rain keep us home. Sarah and I had planned a date to celebrate our third year together as boyfriend and girlfriend. I wasn't going to miss that. Wearing my best dress slacks, a button-down shirt and a blazer I'd borrowed from my father's closet, I left my house and drove to town. I had a bouquet of red roses, a necklace and a reservation at the restaurant where we'd had our first date."

He drew in a deep breath and let it out slowly before continuing.

Savvie sat quietly, listening without comment.

"I showed up at her house in my pickup. Her father mentioned that the weatherman predicted the rain would turn to freezing rain, and that I should get Sarah home before that happened." His lips pressed together. "I promised I would."

Savvie's chest tightened, already guessing he hadn't kept his promise.

"We went to the restaurant. I gave her the flowers and the gift. When our meal came, I overheard the wait staff whispering to each other that the weather was getting bad, and they might have to close early." He shook his head. "I blew it off. We finished our dinner. When we left the restaurant, the sidewalk out front was a little slippery. Sarah nearly fell, but I caught her, and we made it to the car without further incident.

"It wasn't until we left town that I realized how slippery the road was getting. But I'd promised to get Sarah home. She lived a couple of miles out of town in the opposite direction from my folks' place on a road that curved through the hills. As I approached a particularly sharp curve, I pressed the brake to slow the vehicle. I wasn't going very fast, but I hit a patch of black ice. The truck spun, sliding off the shoulder, down an embankment and into a pond." Hunter's voice grew ragged.

Savvie's breath lodged in her lungs.

"The front of the truck dipped down into the water. For a brief moment, I thought it would float. But then it sank into the icy water. I knew we had to get out before the cab filled completely. It was coming in fast and was bitterly cold, stealing my breath away.

"Once the engine submerged, it died, and the interior of the cab went dark. I struggled to unbuckle my seatbelt, finally getting it to release.

"Sarah couldn't find hers. I reached across the console and pressed the button. It didn't disengage. The water rose to our chests. I was floating, but Sarah was trapped in her seat. When I reached into my pocket for the knife I carried everywhere but at school, I realized I'd left it at home in the jeans I changed out of earlier.

"I couldn't cut the belt, the button wouldn't release and the water had filled the cab up to Sarah's neck. Knowing I only had seconds, I pushed hard on the driver's side door. It wouldn't budge. I pressed the button to lower the window. It didn't work. I leaned across Sarah and shoved against her door. The water on the inside had equalized with the water on the outside of the truck, allowing the door to swing open.

"I pulled myself across Sarah, out her door and swam to the surface. I could see lights passing on the highway at the top of the embankment. If I could get someone to stop, maybe they'd have a knife. I dragged myself up the slippery slope to the highway.

"The clock was ticking. I knew that by then, the cab would be full, and Sarah would be underwater. Not a single vehicle appeared. I waited one excruciating minute. No headlights appeared. The freezing rain was accumulating on the road, in my hair and clung to my damp clothing. I dove back into the pond, swam down to the truck and tried again to get the buckle to release. Nothing I did worked. I tugged at the belt, trying to loosen it from across her lap, but it was tight, having cinched close when the truck had bumped down the embankment and hit the water.

"I stayed down as long as I could, then swam to the surface, took a breath and went back down. The cold slowed my movements and made it hard for my hands to clasp the seatbelt buckle.

"Sarah had gone limp. I could do nothing to free her. But I knew I had to try. I couldn't leave her. Once again, I swam to the surface and dragged myself up the embankment.

"Headlights shone from around the curve. I stepped out into the middle of the road, half-frozen, not giving a damn if the oncoming vehicle hit me. It was moving as if in slow motion and stopped in the gravel on the narrow shoulder of the road.

"A man jumped out. I begged him for a knife so I could get Sarah out of the truck. He handed me a flashlight and told me to shine the light into the pond. I slid down the embankment behind him. The man dove into the pond; I tried to follow but could barely move. I shined the light at the point where bubbles rose and prayed.

"After what seemed like forever, the man surfaced, his hand on the back of Sarah's jacket, pulling her up behind him."

Hunter looked into Savvie's face, his brown eyes nearly black with grief.

Savvie's heart pinched hard in her chest.

"She was blue and lifeless." He stared down at his hands. "It was too late. She was gone."

Savvie sat beside Hunter in silence, her heart aching for the eighteen-year-old whose first brush with death had been so tragic.

"I still have nightmares where I see her beautiful blue face, hovering in the water like a ghost." He rested his hands on his knees and drew in a deep breath, letting it out slowly.

Savvie nodded. "I still have nightmares where my stepfather is a raging bull, charging toward me. Or of my mother staring at me, her words echoing in my head. *What have you done?*" She laid her hand over his and squeezed gently. "Hunter, you didn't kill Sarah."

"I didn't save her," he bit out.

"You tried." Her words meant nothing to the man. Trying hadn't kept his girl alive.

"I shouldn't have taken her out in such bad weather. It was my fault she died that night. I should've died with her. So many times, I wished I had."

"Is that why you joined the military instead of going to college?" she asked.

He nodded. "I had to get out of my hometown. I couldn't face Sarah's family. They were devastated. I couldn't look into her father's eyes. Because I broke my promise to him, his daughter was dead. Because I broke that promise, I killed her."

"You didn't kill her," Savvie insisted. "It was an accident."

Hunter pushed to his feet and paced the length of the barn.

Savvie stood but didn't join him. He'd just unloaded the burden of his past on her. He needed to walk it off and collect himself.

After several more passes, he stopped in front of her.

"I'm sorry," he said.

"For what?" she asked.

"You didn't need to hear all that. It's my problem, not yours."

Savvie stood and touched a hand to his chest. "Thank you for trusting me to hear it." She gave him a crooked smile. "We have something in common."

He captured the hand resting on his chest. "That we both killed someone when we were teens? Not exactly a commonality I'd like to claim."

"No. At a tender age, we both experienced hugely traumatic events that changed our lives forever."

Hunter's fingers closed around hers. He brought her hand up to his mouth and brushed his lips across the backs of her knuckles. "That makes us equally damaged. Is that supposed to be a good thing?"

"I think so." She wrapped her other hand around his neck, leaned up on her toes and whispered against his lips, "It helps me to understand you better."

His brow dipped. "How so?"

She leaned into him. "For instance, I can tell you really want to kiss me, but you don't want me to think anything between us could be any more than a brief fling." Savvie leaned forward and brushed her lips across his. "Don't worry. I could never have anything more than a brief fling. My life isn't my own; it hasn't been since I joined the organization. And just so you know…a brief fling sounds amazing. I hope you will consider it."

His lips curved into a genuine smile. "Are you propositioning me?"

She chuckled. "I guess I am. I have no expectations of becoming the future Mrs. Falcon or the future Mrs. Anyone Else. A fling would be good."

Hunter laughed. "I can't keep up with the way you think."

"That's how I maintain the mystery." She patted her hand against his chest. "As much as I want to leap into that fling, we should save that proposition for later. Right now, I say we check in on Kyla and Swede. Surely, they've found something or have gotten my internet access up and running. I need to help." Her brow puckered. "Are you ready?"

His lips twisted. "As ready as ever. Although your proposal intrigues me."

Savvie turned and started up the stairs, glad for an excuse to have her back to him. At least he wouldn't see her cheeks burn a bright red.

Had she really just propositioned the man?

Now that she had, did she want to go through with it?

Oh, hell yeah!

Then why wasn't she heading back to their rooms instead of climbing the steps to the war room, where they might be there for hours?

Because now that she'd expressed her desire to engage in something sexy, she found herself suddenly shy.

What the ever-lovin' fuck had gotten into her?

Well, making love with Hunter wouldn't happen anytime soon. Not until they found the women.

Their lives ranked higher than Savvie's pathetic excuse for a love life.

Only after they'd found the others and gotten them to safety could Savvie indulge in something that might satisfy the itch Hunter inspired. And then, it would only be a short fling. She'd move on soon after. She couldn't let her past work plague Hunter and the rest of his team.

When she pushed through the door into the war room, Stone and Kyla looked up from a single computer monitor they had both been studying.

"Oh, good," Kyla said. "Stone was just about to come get you."

"Were you able to set me up with a computer and internet access?"

Kyla nodded. "The final app is loaded. The laptop is ready for your use. But that's not the big news." She nodded toward the monitor. "Swede's contact thinks he has something."

Savvie and Hunter hurried forward.

"Did they find the other captives?" Savvie's pulse raced as she stared at the monitor.

Swede's face appeared. "Savvie."

Savvie nodded. "Swede."

Hunter stepped up beside Savvie. "Anything yet on the whereabouts of the people Marcus was collecting?"

Swede nodded. "We think so."

Savvie reached for Hunter's hand. "Where?"

"In Miami," Swede responded. "One of my dark web informants contacted me less than an hour ago with a warehouse address."

Savvie squeezed Hunter's hand. "We have to go."

Swede shook his head. "It'll take too long for any of us here in Montana, or our Colorado division, to get there. However, Chuck, one of our team from here in Eagle Rock, is on vacation in Miami with his wife and daughter. We've sent him to check on the location."

Savvie's chest tightened. "Alone?"

Hank appeared on the monitor. "He's taking the lead just to check out the location. I notified my connection with the FBI. He's pulling together a task force to investigate the building and the Caldwell operations."

"No, no, no," Savvie murmured. "When did you notify the FBI?"

"As soon as I got an address. I've been working with them since our last conversation a couple of hours ago."

Savvie's shoulders sagged. "If those people were in that warehouse, they're gone now."

Hank frowned. "My contact with the FBI can be trusted. He assured me he would build a task force without informing them of their intended target until they deploy. He's the only one I've communicated with about the Caldwell's involvement in the human trafficking ring."

Savvie's lips firmed into a tight line. "Swede, has your firewall experienced any hits during the past few hours?"

He nodded. "A few. The firewall blocked them every time."

"They know you're looking for them," Savvie said. "They have enough money and access to the best hackers to protect their operation and shut down anyone who might pose a threat."

"I did not inform my contact with the FBI that I was sending one of my men in. We instructed Chuck to observe, not engage," Hank said. "He should be getting close to the location now."

Though Hank and Swede's faces were still on the monitor, they appeared to be looking at something else.

"He's almost there," Swede reported. "We're tracking his cell phone."

"Please tell me he didn't take his wife and daughter," Savvie whispered.

"He didn't," Hank assured her. "He's there now. We should be hearing from him soon."

Swede blinked. "What the—"

Savvie's breath caught and held.

Hank's face darkened. "Chuck's location dot on the map disappeared."

Swede's eyebrows pulled together to form a V. For a long moment, the only sound coming through the monitor was that of fingers tapping on a keyboard.

"I tried to text him," Swede said. "It didn't deliver. His phone appears to be offline."

More tapping on the keyboard sounded, and Swede's frown deepened. "Fuck."

"What?" Savvie's heart raced. She wanted to be there with Swede and Hank, seeing whatever they were looking at.

Hank laid a hand on Swede's shoulder. "I'll have them get the plane ready." The head of Brotherhood Protectors pulled his cell phone from his pocket and turned away.

Swede scrubbed a hand over his face and turned toward Stone, Kyla, Hunter and Savvie. "I tapped into the 911 calls in Miami. There've been numerous reports of a major explosion in the warehouse district. Right around the address we sent Chuck to investigate."

Savvie pressed a hand to her gut. "If Hank's getting a plane ready to go to Miami, I want to be on it."

CHAPTER 10

HUNTER HELD onto Savvie's hand, though his focus was on Swede and Hank several hours away from them, but still right there in the same room through technology.

He'd met Chuck Johnson. He was the old man of the Brotherhood Protectors. An ex-Navy SEAL, he'd also worked for the FBI. His little girl had been born right around the same time as Hank's little guy, McClain.

Chuck was a good guy. The thought of him being hurt by the explosion made Hunter's blood boil.

"Any reports from first responders?" Savvie asked.

"Nothing yet," Swede reported.

Hank turned back to face Swede while still talking on his phone. "Hold, please, I have another call coming in." Hank lowered his cell phone and checked the screen, a frown pulling his eyebrows together. He showed the number to Swede, shrugged and answered the call. "This is Hank."

As he listened to the caller, his frown cleared, and a relieved smile replaced it. "Thank God." Hank grinned in the monitor. "It's Chuck. He's okay, but his phone was broken in the explosion." He listened again and nodded. "Thanks for the update. We were worried about you. Let the EMTs check you over. You don't want to step on a cruise ship with a potential concussion. Keep us posted."

Hank ended the call and nodded, smiling. "That's a relief." He raked a hand through his hair. "The explosion threw him a few feet. To brace for the fall, he flung his cell phone. It hit a wall and shattered. He had to borrow a phone from one of the first responders to call us. I'm glad he did."

Hunter let go of the breath he hadn't realized he'd been holding. "Good to hear."

"I'm glad Chuck's all right," Savvie said. "Did he have the opportunity to scope the warehouse before the explosion?"

Hank nodded. "Not much, but enough to know it was empty."

"That doesn't make sense." Savvie tilted her head. "We need to think like one of the Caldwells."

"Why destroy the warehouse if you've already cleared it?" Hunter mused aloud.

"Maybe they set out to lure would-be rescuers in," Kyla offered. "They might want to identify people they need to keep an eye on to limit disruptions in their shipments."

"Especially now that they know someone is actively looking for them." Savvie's jaw hardened. "It will be even harder to sneak up on them. If the warehouse had been used to stage their victims, it might mean they've shipped them to their destinations."

Hunter's brow wrinkled. "Savvie, didn't you say Marcus told his contact to include you with the others? That means that, as of last night, they hadn't been shipped."

Savvie dipped her head. "He also said I'd get a good price, which means they were *anticipating* sales, not that they were filling orders."

Stone's eyes narrowed. "Given the upset caused by the death of Marcus Caldwell and the subsequent manhunt for his killer, they might want to lay low with their product."

"With all eyes on the Caldwells," Hunter said, "their buyers might be hesitant to step forward until the furor dies down."

Savvie huffed out a breath. "All hopeful speculation. We need facts. We need boots on the ground in Miami." She met Hank's gaze on the monitor. "Were you able to secure a plane for the flight to Miami?"

Hank crossed his arms over his chest. "Unfortunately, not for a few days. My pilot put the plane in the shop for its annual checkup. It'll be no less than four days before it's ready, and only if they can get started right away."

"Commercial flights?" Kyla's hands hovered over the keyboard. "I can book seats on the next flight out of Bozeman."

"You might book flights for others..." Stone pinned Kyla with a stern glance, "but you're not going anywhere. You're too close to your due date to fly back and forth to Florida. I shouldn't have let you go the first time."

Kyla's lips pursed. "You didn't *let* me go. I *chose* to go."

"Okay, you *chose* to go." Stone's lips tipped upward at the corners. "I should've highly discouraged you from making that choice."

Hank leaned closer to the monitor. "I agree with Stone. Kyla, you need to stay put, if not to keep the baby safe, then to keep Stone safe. He'd worry about you the entire time instead of focusing on the mission. For that matter, Kyla, why don't you come up to Eagle Rock? You can stay at the ranch. Sadie would love the company. She'll be back from LA the day after tomorrow. They're wrapping up her latest film today."

Kyla's brow dipped low. "I'm pregnant, not an invalid. I love Sadie, but I'd go nuts sitting around with nothing to do but chat. I'm used to going ninety miles an hour, even if it's sitting at a computer all day."

"You could hang out with Swede," Stone suggested.

Kyla glared at Stone. "I don't need a babysitter."

Stone raised an eyebrow. "He might teach you some of his hacking skills."

Kyla's eyes narrowed. "That would only carry me for a couple of hours, not a couple of days. If I'm to be grounded, I'd rather stay here and continue to surf the internet and help around the lodge."

Stone grinned. "My father and Cookie would appreciate some assistance."

"And you can leave me behind and go on a mission without the burden of your pregnant wife." She snorted. "Fine. I'll stay. As long as you find those women, free them and get back here before I go into labor."

"Deal." Stone winked.

Hunter studied Stone and Kyla's struggle. He realized Stone wasn't trying to be overbearing. The man really cared about Kyla and their baby. He loved her, and she loved him.

Surprisingly envious, Hunter wondered what it would feel like to be loved that much. His gaze went to Savvie. What would it be like to love Savvie as much as Stone loved Kyla?

Easy. What wasn't to love about the retired assassin? She'd defended her mother when she'd been beaten so badly by a man who'd promised to love, honor and cherish her. Now, Savvie was doggedly determined to save the other captives before they were sold into the sex-slave trade. She didn't have to. She wanted to.

No. She was *driven* to free them.

"While we wait for a plane to get us to Miami, we need Kyla and Swede to find where they've taken the captives," Hank was saying.

Savvie heaved a sigh. "Wouldn't it be easier to go to Miami and look for ourselves?"

"You have dedicated internet here with a firewall to keep others from tracing you," Swede said. "If I thought it would be easier to go to Miami to find those people, I'd be all for it. But think about it; Miami is a big city with lots of people who could be working for the Caldwells and lots of places they could hide their captives. The needle in a haystack comes to mind. At least from here, with excellent access to the internet, we can conduct our search safely."

Hunter nodded. "And no one will be trying to run you down, shoot at you or slip drugs into your drink."

"But we're much slower to react from here," Savvie argued. "A four-hour plane ride gives them the advantage. You can move a lot of people to a lot of different places in four hours."

"True," Hank said. "Keep searching the internet. I'll work on getting a plane sooner than four days. I'd prefer not to fly commercial, especially if they're onto us."

"Jump in, Savvie," Kyla waved toward a laptop opened on a counter with a large monitor mounted on the wall. "You're all set with internet access. You can help."

Savvie drew in a breath and let it out slowly. "Great."

"It'll take all three of us to find someone who knows where they're being held."

"Then let's get started." Savvie released Hunter's hand, pulled out a chair in front of the laptop and sank into it. After the first few minutes of familiarizing herself with the hardware, she settled into the task, head down, fingers flying.

Hunter met Stone's gaze. "If I thought I could help with the online search, I would. But I'd just slow these computer gurus down with too many questions."

Stone nodded. "I've accepted my technical limitations. Kyla can run circles around me on a computer." He turned to the monitor. "Anything we can do in the meantime?"

Hank nodded. "Have your team ready to roll. I'll put my guys on alert."

"Will do," Stone said. "We'll be ready whenever you say the word."

Hank turned to his computer guy. "Swede, are you going to keep this video link running?"

The blond Viking waved a hand without looking up. "Not necessary until one of us comes up with something we can run with."

Hank looked up. "Then we're out here."

"Out here," Stone repeated.

The monitor blinked off.

Stone motioned for Hunter to follow him into the armory, a room dedicated to storing all the weapons available to the team. "We might as well stage what we need if we end up deploying the entire team."

Stone notified Dax Young and Carter Manning to head their way. Dax had moved in with Amanda Small on the Wind River Reservation in Wyoming, a couple hour's drive from West Yellowstone. Carter Manning was currently in Washington DC with Wyoming's congresswoman, Liliana Light-feather.

While Stone spoke with Dax and Carter, Hunter texted Bubba Yates and Moe Cleveland, asking them to report to the war room. When they arrived, Hunter and Stone brought them up to speed on what had happened in Miami.

The four men spent the next few hours going through weapons, ammunition and armor-plated vests. They tested communications and tracking devices. For each member of the Yellowstone team, they packed go-bags with everything they might need for a rescue operation.

For lunch, Cookie brought a tray of sandwiches,

and John Jacobs carried pitchers of tea and lemonade.

Kyla and Savvie had put feelers out to their contacts. None had responded so far.

As sunshine waned into dusk, Stone and his packing team had done all they could to prepare. They left the go-bags stacked in a corner of the war room and descended into the barn below. Bubba and Moe returned to the lodge to help Cookie with dinner preparations while Stone and Hunter stayed to care for the horses.

Hunter filled two buckets with grain. He hung one bucket in the stall with Frisco. Stone brought in a section of hay.

As Hunter was hanging the second bucket in Duchess's stall, the lights overhead blinked out.

"What the hell?" Stone muttered from somewhere outside the stall.

The door opened to the loft.

"Hey, anyone down there?" Savvie's voice called out.

"Stone and I are," Hunter turned on his cell phone's flashlight and shined it toward the stairs. Unfortunately, the beam didn't get very far. "Lights out up there?"

"Everything's out," Savvie said.

"Even the computers?" Stone asked.

"Everything," Savvie repeated.

"The battery backups should power them. They

should still be running," Stone turned on his cell phone flashlight and located a battery-powered lantern hanging from a hook. When he switched it on, the lantern spread a soft glow throughout the lower level of the barn. "I'll check the breakers." He strode into the tack room, carrying the lantern.

After a couple of loud clicks, the lights blinked back on.

Stone emerged, shaking his head. "They hadn't been flipped. I don't know why everything shut down."

"Whatever you did worked down here," Hunter said.

Moe and Bubba entered the barn.

"Did you lose power out here," Bubba asked.

"We did," Stone said. "I flipped the breakers, and it came back on."

Moe nodded. "Same in the lodge."

Still carrying the lantern, Stone strode for the stairs. "Let's see if they're fully operational in the war room."

Stone took the steps two at a time and flung open the door at the top.

All the lights were on.

Kyla and Savvie stood side by side, staring down at the monitor at Savvie's workstation.

"Not good," Savvie said.

"Very not good," Kyla agreed.

"What's not good?" Hunter stepped up behind them and stared at the monitor.

The screen was black with neon yellow words flashing across the middle.

BACK OFF OR ELSE

"That's what came up when I restarted the unit," Savvie said.

Kyla snorted. "Well, that's rude."

A moment later, the words were replaced with a deluge of numbers and letters scrolling across the screen.

Savvie touched the delete key on the keyboard.

Nothing happened.

She tried the reboot command.

Nothing.

Kyla reached across Savvie's hands, pressed the on-off button and held it down until the annoying scroll of numbers and letters faded to black.

She waited a few seconds and then pressed the button to restart the machine.

After a couple of minutes, the screen blinked to life.

WELCOME TO OR ELSE

A phone rang near Kyla's workstation. She crossed to her desk, searched for the device and lifted a clunky receiver, her eyebrows descending. "It's the satellite phone." She pressed it to her ear. "Hello." Her frown eased. "Swede? Yes. This is Kyla. Man, we have a problem here." She listened, her eyebrows forming a deep V over her nose. "You too? Bastards! What do we do now?" She nodded. "Okay. I'm putting you on speaker to free my hands."

She hit the speaker button and laid the satellite phone on the tabletop.

"Have you flipped the breakers?" Swede asked.

"We have," Stone said. "The electricity came back on. Should we flip it off and on again?"

"Yes," Swede said. "Maybe it will reset all the units."

"Did it work for you?" Savvie asked. "Did rebooting clear the bug?"

"No. But we can hope it will work for you, though I don't hold out hope that it will." Swede's voice was tight.

"What happened? Why did our computers go down?" Savvie asked.

"They got past the firewall," Swede said.

Kyla muttered a curse. "How the hell did they do that?"

"I don't know, but we need to get back up and running," Swede said. "I'd just received some intel from a source in Miami when everything cut off."

"Intel about what?" Savvie asked.

"A possible location where they'd seen trucks delivering cargo in the dead of night."

"Where?" Hunter and Savvie demanded as one.

"I didn't get that far before everything crashed," Swede said. "Everything here is tied to our computer security system. Door locks, gate openers, electricity, computers. I did a manual reboot of the breakers, so at least we have power."

"That's what happened here," Stone said. "Did you get the same message when you tried to log into your computers?"

"*Back off or else*," Swede said. "And when I rebooted the network, I got *Welcome to Or Else.*"

"What's Hank's take on all this?" Stone asked.

"I don't know," Swede said. "He was headed out to check on a mare with a limp. Said he'd be right back." A pause. "Wait. Here he comes."

"Swede," Hank's voice sounded in the background. "I need you to bring up the phone number for the security company providing Sadie and the kids' protection in LA. The number I have says it's disconnected, and Sadie's cell is telling me she's offline."

"That's not good," Swede said. "Our computers and cell phones are down. I have no way of looking up the numbers you're asking for."

Hunter's gut knotted. The seemingly separate incidences weren't coincidental.

"Kyla, I'm putting you on hold. I've got an incoming call," Swede said.

Silence filled the room like a scream.

"They really don't want us to find the other captives," Savvie murmured.

"They're threatening us," Stone noted.

Hank's voice came back on the satellite phone. "That was Sadie."

"Sweet Jesus," Kyla breathed. "Is she—"

"She's all right, and so are Emma and McClain. Their cell phones were compromised. Plus, someone broke into Sadie's dressing room and left a message on her makeup mirror."

"Back off or else?" Kyla proffered.

"Right. They're making sure we pay attention." Hank's tone was tight, his words clipped. "And I can tell you...they have my full attention."

"And mine," Swede added. "I have a laptop that wasn't connected to the system when everything went down. I'll take it into town. The Blue Moose Tavern has WIFI. I'll get in touch with my contact and see what he has."

"I contacted one of the celebrities we've done work for," Hank said. "He operates his own 707 and is willing to fly our team to Miami. All we have to do is let him know when."

"On my way to Eagle Rock," Swede said.

"I'm going with him," Hank announced. "I have my team here on standby. Kujo, Talon and Boomer are prepping go-bags. We'll have at least seven ready to roll once we say the word."

"Our six are packed. Two are inbound on the road from Wind River."

"And me," Savvie added. "I'm coming."

"I have the Colorado division on standby if we

need more," Hank said. "We're on our way to find a signal. Will get back to you ASAP."

Hank ended the call.

Stone tried the other computers. Each came up with the same messages. Finally, he turned to the others, all watching him for guidance.

"We might as well go to dinner and get some rest. If we bug out, it could be a very long night."

Savvie closed her laptop.

When Hunter held out his hand, she placed hers in his and walked out of the war room with him, following the others into the lodge.

The long table had been set with plates and cutlery. Cookie emerged from the kitchen carrying a platter filled with roast beef, potatoes and carrots. Tinker followed with a basket full of freshly baked dinner rolls and a bowl filled with a leafy green salad.

The other guests in the dining room had been served and were happily eating.

Hunter held Savvie's chair as she sat at the table.

Breely Brant and Chelsea Youngblood came out of the kitchen carrying pitchers of coffee, tea and lemonade.

Moe introduced Breely to Savvie as his fiancée.

Bubba introduced Chelsea as the love of his life and a wolfologist.

Chelsea laughed as she took her seat at the table. "I'm a biologist who studies the wolves in this area.

Nice to meet you, Savvie." She passed the basket of bread rolls. "What brings you to West Yellowstone?"

"I needed to get out of Miami," Savvie said.

Chelsea exchanged a glance with Breely and nodded knowingly. "Our guys keeping you safe from whoever's causing you grief?" She helped herself to some salad and passed the bowl.

Savvie nodded. "As a matter of fact, yes. They got me out of Miami alive."

"The Brotherhood Protectors are good at what they do." Breely gave Savvie a gentle smile. "I hope things are resolved quickly for you." She took a roll from the basket. "Cookie makes the best bread."

The group at the table discussed the weather, the continuing renovations of rooms at the lodge and Kyla's baby.

Savvie sat quietly, picking at her food, her gaze on the satellite phone lying on the table beside Stone.

Hunter reached beneath the table and captured her hand, squeezing gently.

By the time dinner was over, Savvie's foot was bouncing, and her hand in his clenched and unclenched.

When they rose to carry their plates into the kitchen, Hunter leaned close and whispered, "Let's go for a walk."

"Shouldn't we help with the dishes?" she asked.

"Go on," Stone said behind them. "We'll take care

of these. And don't worry; I'll find you if I hear anything from Hank."

Savvie heaved a sigh. "Thank you. I need to stretch my legs and keep moving."

After leaving their plates in the commercial sink, Hunter led Savvie through the lobby and out the front of the lodge.

The lodge sat on the western edge of West Yellowstone. Hunter walked with Savvie, heading east into town. He held her hand, letting the silence stretch between them. It was a comfortable silence for him. Savvie seemed to relax.

"It's beautiful out here." She drew in a deep breath. "And it smells so clean and fresh. Much better than DC."

He laughed. "That's not hard to do. The traffic in Miami reminded me why I don't want to live in a big city ever again."

Savvie leaned into his shoulder. "Same. I just need to find a job that is low stress. I wonder if I could learn how to make flower arrangements. Or maybe I'll be a dog sitter. I could hug puppies all day long."

"From assassin to dog sitter..." Hunter tipped his head. "Somehow, I don't think it'll be an easy transition."

"No?"

"Like military coming off active duty, they...we... have a hard time fitting into civilian life. Every day deployed was a fight for survival. In the civilian world, most people have never been in a life-or-death battle. They've never been shot at or had mortar rounds lobbed into their sleeping quarters. They've never had a close friend die in their arms."

Hunter stopped and faced her.

"They're more concerned about what to wear out on a date, what car they should buy, or what movie to watch on television. Those things seem so inconsequential to someone who has lived through shelling, shooting—"

"Or abuse," Savvie inserted.

Hunter nodded. "Or abuse. You've lived that life-or-death kind of life with your stepfather and in your work. It's hard to assimilate into a society that will never understand."

She sighed. "Yeah, I get that it won't be easy. But I want to try. I'd rather help people than hurt them."

He nodded. Thus, her desire to save the people being staged for sale into the sex trade.

"I'm lucky," Hunter said. "I didn't think I'd find a place to fit in, where I could be myself and make a difference. But I did find that place."

"With the Brotherhood Protectors?" She looked up into his face.

He nodded. "They get me. We're a team. We have each others' backs. And we're using the skills we'd worked so hard to master while on active duty."

"Do they only hire men?"

"Kyla works for the Brotherhood," Hunter pointed out.

"She works in an office. Would Stone or Hank hire a woman to do the same kind of work you or Stone would do?"

"Yes, he would," Hunter said. "Not that arranging flowers is a bad occupation…"

Savvie chuckled. "I'm keeping an open mind. I might try several jobs before I settle on one. Or maybe, I'll have more than one job. I really like the idea of dog sitting. If I don't do that, I'd like to have a job where I come home every night to a dog of my own. A rescue, or maybe, a senior dog who deserves to live his last days being loved and spoiled."

Hunter turned around to face Savvie. He cupped her cheek with his hand. "You know, you're special."

"How so?" She covered his hand with hers and turned her face to press her lips into his palm.

His heart skipped several beats and then raced to catch up. Her touch was making him crazy, scrambling his thoughts and making it hard for him to focus. "Most people are afraid of change. Nervous of making the wrong choices."

She gave him a twisted smile. "Coming from where I've been, choosing not to change would be a bad choice. Taking a chance on something new is the right choice. I'm ready for some happiness in my life. If I'm afraid of anything, it's that I might not find what makes me happy. I'm willing to keep looking until I do."

"Life's too short to be unhappy." Hunter stared down into her face, warmth spreading through his chest. "You deserve to be happy after all you've been through."

Her forehead puckered. "For years, I didn't think I deserved to be happy."

"You came from an abusive environment." Hunter cupped the back of her neck. "And now?"

"I realized I was the only one who could make me happy, but it wasn't going to happen while I was doing what I was doing. So, I decided to reinvent myself. I'm at that stage where I'm a blank slate. I can be anything."

"You will be the best whatever it is you choose to be, as long as you believe in yourself."

The sun dipped behind the mountain peaks, turning the sky brilliant orange, mauve and purple, bathing the assassin in a muted aura of fading light. She was beautiful, and he wanted to kiss her more than he wanted to take his next breath.

She tipped her head back, her eyelids dropping low. "Are you going to kiss me?"

He nodded. "Damn right, I am."

"About damn time." Savvie rose on her toes.

Hunter lowered his head and claimed her lips, drinking her in like rain to parched earth.

In some ways, they were so very much alike.

She hadn't believed she deserved happiness because she'd killed a man and then had gone into a life as an assassin.

Hunter hadn't believed he deserved happiness because he hadn't saved Sarah from drowning. He'd lived. She hadn't because of his stupid decision to take her on a date in treacherous conditions. His marriage had failed from the moment it had started —all because he hadn't believed he deserved love and happiness.

Yet, he was kissing this woman now, and he'd never felt more alive. Could he let go of the past and dare to let himself be happy?

CHAPTER 11

Savvie leaned back and stared up into Hunter's eyes, her pulse quickening. "Remember that fling I hinted at earlier?"

He cocked an eyebrow. "The proposition?"

She raised a shoulder and let it fall. "Fling... proposition...whatever. It goes back to life's short... We might not have much time together, so why not make the most of it?"

He glanced around at the darkening street. "Here? Now?"

She laughed. "Though lying naked under the stars does have a certain appeal, I'd rather know what I'm lying naked on." She tucked her hand into the crook of his arm before she lost her nerve. "Let's go back to the lodge."

They started back, their pace picking up until

they half-walked and half-ran the remaining hundred yards, laughing as they neared the lodge.

"We should check in with Stone," Hunter said as they entered the lobby.

Thankfully, they didn't have far to go.

Stone stood at the front desk, talking with his father, the satellite phone still in his hand.

When he spotted Hunter and Savvie, he shook his head. "Nothing yet."

Though Savvie wanted to resolve the issue with the captives, she was glad they had a little time before they had to leave.

"We'll be in our rooms," Hunter said.

"Smart," Stone said. "We don't know when we'll leave or how long we'll be gone. You might as well rest now."

Hunter walked with Savvie up the staircase to the second floor. Once they were out of sight of the lobby, they ran the rest of the way to their rooms.

"Mine or yours?" Savvie asked.

"Mine." He slipped his key into the lock and pushed the door wide.

Then Hunter swept Savvie into his arms and carried her across the threshold. Once they were in his room, he kicked the door closed behind him.

Her pulse sent molten hot blood raging through her, pooling low in her belly.

If making love with Hunter was one of those bad

choices, it would be one of the best bad choices she'd ever make.

She had to remind herself that this was not the start of something. Whatever happened with Hunter would only be a brief encounter, not a long-term relationship. Her past would always be a danger to anyone she might grow to care about. If she cared enough, she'd keep moving and not stay with one person long enough that someone would punish him to torture her.

Hunter carried her the short distance to the bed and lowered her legs to the floor. "Still on board?"

She grabbed the hem of her borrowed T-shirt, her eyes narrowing. "Are you?"

He chuckled and pulled her hips up against his. The hard ridge of his desire pressed into her belly. "I'm on board and halfway there."

She gazed up into his eyes. "As long as you understand that what we do together will have no strings attached."

He hesitated for a moment, his brow wrinkling. "Okay." Cupping the back of her head, he leaned in, his lips hovering over hers. "No strings, huh?"

"I could be gone tomorrow," she insisted, even as she rocked up on her toes, closing the distance between their lips. She kissed him briefly. "Even though I've left my line of work, my past could come back to haunt me in the shape of a family member bent on avenging the death of their scumbag relative. Anyone near me could become collateral damage in that attempt at revenge."

"What if the person with you is willing to take the risk?" he asked, pressing his lips to her temple, then moving to that sensitive spot on her neck, just below her ear.

"No strings," she said, her voice barely more than a whisper.

When he brushed his lips so softly against her skin, it left her breathless and ready for more.

With her fingers curled around the T-shirt hem, she dragged it up her torso.

His hands joined hers, raising the shirt higher, exposing her bare breasts, and finally, tugging it over her head.

Not knowing when word would come from Hank and Swede, Savvie didn't waste time. She shucked her shoes and the sweats Hunter had loaned her, kicking them to the side.

Hunter wasn't far behind. When they were both naked, he walked her backward until she bumped into the bed.

He tipped her chin up and brushed his thumb across her lips. "How do you feel about foreplay?"

She cocked an eyebrow. "If done right, it's a game changer."

A slow smile curled the corners of his lips. "Challenge accepted."

"We don't have much time," she reminded him.

"Sweetheart, if done right, it doesn't take much time." He laid her back on the mattress, her legs dangling over the side of the bed. "Think game changer." Hunter claimed her lips in a kiss that ignited her blood, sending it searing through her veins. His tongue pushed past her teeth to caress hers in a sensual, thrusting motion.

Already, Savvie's body ached for more. Her channel was damp and ready for him.

Hunter burned a path of fire down the side of her neck, pausing briefly to flick the thundering pulse at the base of her throat. Moving lower, he brushed his lips across her collarbone, over the swell of her left breast and stopped to capture her nipple between his teeth.

Savvie arched her back, urging him to take more.

He sucked the nipple into his mouth and pulled hard, flicking the beaded tip with his tongue.

Savvie moaned, her fingers slipping into his hair.

He switched to the other breast and teased it until she writhed beneath him.

His hand slid down her belly to the juncture of her thighs, cupping her sex.

Savvie parted her legs, her channel wet and ready.

Abandoning her breast, he trailed kisses down her torso, settling his body between her thighs.

When Hunter parted Savvie's folds, he blew a stream of warm air over her clit.

ELLE JAMES

A shiver shook her. Anticipation reached a fevered pitch.

His tongue flicked her there, sending a shock of electricity straight to her core. When he flicked again, her body trembled with aftershocks, tension building, growing, surging like a tsunami. At first, it rushed over her, then dragged her into the deep end, the ebb and flow of sensations intensifying with each touch.

One last flick sent her catapulting over the edge, launching her into the stratosphere, the afterburners firing all the way.

She rode the rocket to the stars, her body roaring like a powerful engine.

As the power waned, she fell back to earth, another ache pulsing, begging to be eased.

Savvie touched his shoulders, urging him to come up to her.

He climbed her body, his hips settling between her legs, his cock, pressing against her entrance.

And he paused.

On the verge of a second orgasm, Savvie's breath caught and held.

"Please," she whispered.

Pulling away from her, he leaned toward the nightstand, yanked open the drawer and fished inside. Precious moments later, his hand surfaced triumphantly with a condom.

He tore it open and rolled it over his shaft before

resuming his position between her legs, the tip of cock nudging her entrance.

Savvie curled her hands around his hips, digging her fingertips into his tight ass.

He dipped in and pulled back out.

"Oh, no, no, no." Her fingers tightened, pulling him into her. All the way.

Coated in her juices, he slid in and out of her, moving slowly at first, then increasing his speed with each pass.

Soon, he was pumping in and out of her.

Savvie raised her knees, planting her heels into the mattress so that she could rise to meet his every thrust.

He pounded harder, moving faster until he slammed into her once more, burying himself to the hilt. He dropped down on top of her, his cock pulsing inside her. For a long moment, he held steady, his body tense, his hips rocking ever so slightly in residual thrusts.

Eventually, he rolled to his side, taking her with him to hold in the crook of his arm as he nuzzled her neck.

Savvie lay with him skin-to-skin, basking in the afterglow of the best sex she'd ever experienced. The man had skills beyond the battlefield.

A dull ache settled in her chest. They'd been good in bed. So good, Savvie would have a hard time forgetting just how good he was. She'd insisted on no strings attached, and she would follow through accordingly.

For a long time after, Savvie lay in the warmth and strength of Hunter's embrace, not wanting to sleep because she'd miss being with him.

Sometime in the night, she must have fallen asleep. A loud knock sounded on the door to Hunter's room, jerking her awake from a deep sleep.

Hunter sat up straight, swung his legs over the opposite side and stood. He grabbed a pair of shorts and dragged them up his legs.

Savvie dove out of bed, scooped her clothes off the floor and moved into the adjoining bathroom, closing the door with a soft snick.

Deep voices rumbled on the other side of the wooden door panel.

Savvie pulled Hunter's T-shirt over her head and let the hem fall below her hips and buttocks. The important stuff was covered. Still, she didn't want to leave the bathroom until whoever had come to Hunter's room was gone. Only then would she slip into her own room, where she hoped Kyla had come through with clothes that fit better than the soft T-shirt and sweats Hunter had provided.

Savvie pressed her ear to the door panel. The voices had grown quiet.

A few moments later, a tap on the other side of the door made her jump.

"All clear," Hunter said.

She opened the door and peered out.

The bedroom door was closed. She and Hunter were alone.

"Who was it?" she asked.

"Stone." Hunter spun toward the dresser against the wall, yanked open the third drawer and pulled out a black T-shirt. He turned to face her while pulling the shirt over his head and down his chest. "We roll in fifteen minutes. Can you be ready?"

Her heart leaped and pounded against her ribs. "They found the captives?" She located the sweatpants she'd kicked aside the night before and jammed her feet into the legs.

"Yes. They're on a private island in the Florida Keys. Hank's friend will get us to Miami. We'll be transported the rest of the way by boat."

"I can be ready in three minutes." Savvie hurried across the room. As she reached for the doorknob, a hand caught her arm and turned her.

She looked up into Hunter's dark brown eyes, her heart melting.

"We're not done," he said.

She frowned. "I don't know what you mean."

"I'm not totally on board with the no strings attached rule. What if I want strings?"

Savvie's heart constricted. "Now isn't the time to discuss this." When she tried to open the door, he leaned his hand against it, holding it closed.

"Just so you know, I'm not giving up on you."

"Hunter." Savvie touched a hand to his chest. "I'll always be looking over my shoulder just to stay alive. Anyone who gets involved with me will be a target. Because. Of. Me." She slid her hands up his chest to circle behind his neck. "Whatever's happening between us can't continue. Because of the choice I made, I'm destined to live alone and move a lot. I don't wish that life on anyone."

"You don't have to keep moving. You can stay here." Hunter gripped her hips and brought them flush against his. "And you don't have to worry about me. I can take care of myself."

"That's not the point." With him standing so close, she couldn't think straight. "Oh, hell, I forgot the point." She lifted up, kissed him hard and fast and dropped back down. "We can talk about this after we rescue the others."

"Damn right, we will," he said.

As she started to back away, he caught the back of her head and kissed her so thoroughly she forgot to breathe.

Hunter broke the kiss as suddenly as he'd initiated it. Then he opened the door and poked his head out into the hallway. "All clear."

Savvie darted out, dug the key from her pocket and fumbled to unlock the door, dropping the key in the process.

Hunter retrieved the key before she could and unlocked her door. "You liked that kiss, didn't you?"

"Too damned much," she murmured and then dove into her room, slamming the door closed behind her.

Soft laughter sounded from the hallway.

"What's wrong with me?" she whispered. "I'm a goddamn assassin, not a silly teenager getting her first kiss."

"It's because that was a damned good kiss," Hunter's voice sounded through the door.

Savvie's lips twitched. "Yes, it was." She raised her fingers to her lips still tingling from his touch. Then she frowned. "But it doesn't change anything."

"It changes everything," Hunter said. Footsteps sounded, and a door closed nearby.

For a long moment, Savvie stood still, letting Hunter's words sink in.

He was right. That kiss...making love...with Hunter...had changed everything.

She was falling for the guy. Never in her career as an assassin had she fallen in love with anyone. She'd kept her distance, breaking off any relationship heading into more serious feelings. On the guy's part, not hers. Savvie knew what was at stake and wouldn't let herself love someone for fear of placing him in the crosshairs of anyone gunning for her.

Then again, she hadn't met anyone as physically strong or combat-ready as Hunter.

No, she hadn't met anyone for whom she had strong feelings. No one she cared enough about to want the life she'd never dreamed possible for her—one in which she and her "forever" partner could build a life together, complete with a kid or two.

Children scared Savvie. Babies, especially. They were so small and completely dependent on others to care for them. Savvie could barely take care of herself. She couldn't begin to take care of the needs of an infant.

Could she?

"Don't be an idiot," Savvie scolded herself, pushed away from the door and headed for the stack of clothing laid out on the bed. Kyla had come through for her once again.

She'd delivered a small collection of outfits, including a couple of pairs of blue jeans, a dress, several tops and a lacy black bra. Also, among the gently worn clothes was a new package of bikini panties in various pastel colors.

Savvie grinned, grabbed black jeans and a black, long-sleeved T-shirt, and quickly changed out of the sweatpants into Kyla's borrowed garments. Though Kyla was a little taller than Savvie, the clothes fit surprisingly well. She'd even included a black elastic ponytail holder and ball cap.

Once dressed, she checked her backpack for her .40 caliber pistol and the extra magazines. She tucked them all back into the backpack and slung it over one shoulder.

When she pulled open her door, Hunter stood there with his fist raised to knock.

"Good," he said. "You're ready."

She followed him down the stairs to the lobby where the team had congregated.

Stone lifted his chin when they joined the group. "Savvie," he pointed to a man with brown hair and blue eyes, "Dax Young." Then Stone waved his hand toward another man with brown hair and brown eyes. "And that's Carter Manning. They've been briefed on what's happened so far and what's at stake. The vehicles are loaded. We're meeting Hank and his guys at the airport in Bozeman. Let's load up."

The men filed out of the lobby into the gray light of predawn.

Stone turned to his pregnant wife. "I'll be back as soon as possible." He kissed her hard and held her close for a long moment. When he stepped back, he bent and pressed his lips to her swollen belly. "See you later, baby. Take care of your mama." He left the lobby, following the others outside.

Savvie followed Hunter and Stone across the lobby.

"Savvie," Kyla called out.

Savvie stopped, turned and met Kyla's gaze.

Kyla's hand rested on her belly, a frown denting her forehead. "Watch out for him, will ya?"

"I will," Savvie promised, her heart pinching tightly in her chest.

Kyla, a trained assassin who could take down a man twice her size without breaking a sweat, looked more vulnerable than Savvie had ever seen her.

"You love him, don't you?" Savvie said.

"More than you could possibly imagine," Kyla admitted.

Savvie's eyes narrowed. "Aren't you afraid that your past could come back to haunt you and, in turn, Stone?"

"Every day of my life," Kyla said. "It was never in my plan to commit to a man. What man could put up with me? I'm headstrong. I speak my mind and don't let anyone push me around. But mostly, what man would accept me or understand my past career?"

Savvie smiled. "Stone."

"He's a keeper. So, bring him back to me and our baby." Tears slipped down her cheeks. "Oh, fuck. I never cry. Except when I'm pregnant. All the hormones going bananas." She hugged Savvie. "Go. Keep our guys safe."

Savvie started to turn.

"And Savvie, you can have a life after the organization. Don't be afraid to go for it."

Savvie dashed out of the lodge, Kyla's words reverberating in her mind.

Hunter stood beside a dark SUV, holding the rear door open.

Savvie dove in and scooted across the seat, making room for Hunter. He stepped in, closed the door and the man named Dax drove them out of the lodge parking lot. A second SUV followed.

Stone sat in the front seat, speaking quietly with Dax, asking him questions about Congresswoman Liliana Lightfeather, the Native American who'd won the congressional seat for the state of Wyoming.

"What did Kyla have to say?" Hunter whispered.

"She wanted me to keep Stone safe for her and the baby." Savvie smiled. "I never could've pictured Kyla head over heels for a man, much less pregnant. It still blows my mind. We were all dedicated to the job. The drill instructors told us the job would be our lives. Forget about having friends and family. It was easier to limit the number of people who know you. The best assassins were the ones who did the job and disappeared back into the woodwork."

"And Kyla broke all the rules, didn't she?"

Savvie nodded. "I've never seen her happier."

"Proving it can be done." Hunter turned to her and took her hands in his. "She's started a new life that doesn't include killing people. And she's let someone into that life." Hunter continued, "If she can do it…"

"So can I?" Savvie shook her head.

"Why not?" Hunter persisted.

"I'm not Kyla," Savvie whispered. "Please. Can we couch this discussion for after we save the Caldwell captives?"

Hunter frowned. He opened his mouth, closed it

and nodded. "Okay. But I repeat, I'm not ready to give up on you, Savvie."

"Duly noted," Savvie said, her heart warming. For a man who'd only just met her, he was staking his claim, or better put, voicing his intent.

Hunter had done a three-hundred-and-sixty-degree turn from what he'd explained about his life the previous day. He was a man who'd avoided commitment because he couldn't forgive himself for not saving his high school sweetheart.

Why had he changed?

Was it her?

Her heart fluttered.

Making love with Hunter had been amazing. Did she want to do it again?

Hell, yes!

The only thing that could have made their time together better would have been more time.

Time to bask in the glow of the best sex Savvie had ever had. Time to explore more of each other's bodies. Time to get to talk and get to know each other better.

Since meeting Hunter, Savvie felt like they'd been running as fast as they could.

Time was running out for the people the Caldwell mafia had captured for sale to others.

Those people needed her focus and the help of the Brotherhood Protectors to free them.

Savvie pushed thoughts of making love with

Hunter to the back of her mind and went over everything she knew about the Caldwells and their nefar-
ious tactics.

When they reached the airport in Bozeman, Dax
drove up to a gate. It opened, and they were able to
drive out onto the tarmac, where a large plane stood
with a portable staircase pushed up to the door.

Hank Patterson appeared at the top of the stairs
and hurried down, along with a couple of other men.

The go-bags were unloaded from the backs of the
SUVs and carried up into the plane.

The pilot made a brief appearance. Savvie recognized him immediately as an actor who had played
an international spy in action-adventure movies.

He disappeared into the cockpit.

Savvie marveled at Hank's friends. Hunter had
mentioned that Hank was married to Sadie McClain,
the megastar with numerous screen credits under
her belt.

The stairs were rolled away, and the door to the
aircraft was closed and secured.

Hank quickly introduced the men he'd brought
with him from Eagle Rock.

Already overwhelmed with names, Savvie nodded
politely and immediately pushed the names to the
back of her mind.

As soon as they had clearance, the pilot taxied to
the end of the runway. Seconds later, the wheels left
the ground.

Her last assignment as an assassin had progressed to a hunt for other victims of the man she'd dispatched. Once they recovered the others, she could move on with her plan to leave killing behind and reinvent Savvie Sanders.

Too bad she couldn't take Hunter with her. Their one night together hadn't nearly been enough.

CHAPTER 12

FOR THE FIRST hour of the flight to Miami, Hank briefed the team on what he and Swede had learned from their contact in Miami.

The items that had been stored in the destroyed warehouse had been moved onto a yacht and transported from Miami to an island near Key West.

The source had given them the coordinates for the island and warned them that the island was heavily guarded by men in speed boats with military-grade rifles mounted on them. The contact warned that the Caldwells had their spies in every government organization. If they tried to send in the Coast Guard, the FBI or the Florida National Guard, the items would disappear before any of those entities would arrive.

The Brotherhood Protectors had to conduct this operation on their own.

Hank and Swede had tapped into surveillance satellites, zeroing in on the coordinates. They had downloaded images of a walled compound on the Atlantic side of the island and a secluded, deep-water cove with a dock. A couple of yachts were moored in the cove with room for more. The dock was manned by two security guards carrying what appeared to be AR-15 rifles.

The rest of the island was covered in thick jungle-like foliage, the outer edges sporting long stretches of sandy beaches.

Hunter studied the images, committing structures and the layout to memory.

They would arrive in Miami during the day, transfer to a yacht and head south to the coordinates, timing their arrival with dusk. The plan was to move in under cover of darkness, breach the compound's wall, locate the prisoners and get them off the island.

Hank's brow furrowed. "It's not much of a plan, considering we don't know what we'll encounter inside the walls of the compound or how many armed guards they have allocated."

"Word from the dark web is that an online art auction is taking place this evening," Swede said. "All products will be shipped out once the auction is complete. Tonight."

"Which means we don't have time to do a thorough reconnaissance prior to moving in," Hank said.

"Any idea how they will ship them out?" Savvie asked.

"One of two ways." Swede pointed to his laptop's screen with the satellite image of the compound and the dock. "They can take them out by boat." He pointed to the walled compound and a large circle within. "Or they could airlift them out by helicopter. As of this image, there wasn't a helicopter on the landing pad. That could change. And the landing pad is large enough for multiple aircraft."

"The yacht getting us to the location will be equipped with two inflatable Zodiacs," Hank said. "The captain will stop far enough out to avoid detection and launch us in the Zodiacs. Then he'll head back out to sea a bit and wait for our radio signal to return.

"We'll make a beach landing on opposite sides of the cove entrance and move to the compound on foot. We'll split up into Eagle Rock and Yellowstone teams. If one team is stalled for any reason, the other can keep moving to the objective."

Hunter reached for Savvie's hand. She was part of the Yellowstone team. He'd keep her close.

Hank leaned back. "For now, you might as well rest and conserve energy. It could be a long day and a longer night."

The men settled back in their seats. Years of special operations missions had conditioned them to take advantage of any downtime to rest. Many closed their eyes and slept.

Hunter sat beside Savvie, still holding her hand. She leaned her head back against the seat and closed her eyes.

For a long time, Hunter studied her, committing her features to memory. She'd secured her shoulder-length, sandy-blond hair in a ponytail at the nape of her neck. Loose tendrils curved around her chin. Her eyebrows, a slightly darker shade than her hair, arched gracefully.

One of them cocked upward as she opened her eyes. "Caught ya," she whispered.

"Busted." He smiled and held up his hands. "Couldn't help myself. You know you're beautiful, don't you?"

She pursed her lips. "Average, at best."

"Nope." He crossed his arms over his chest and leaned his head back. "Nothing average about you."

She chuckled and closed her eyes again. "Whatever. Wake me when we get there."

Hunter dozed off and on for the remainder of the flight. He was fully awake when the plane touched down at a smaller airport south of Miami international airport.

Once the plane taxied to a stop at the FBO, a portable staircase was rolled up to the side of the aircraft.

Hunter and Savvie each grabbed a go-bag,

descended the stairs and crossed the tarmac to the four SUVs lined up for their use.

They loaded equipment into the vehicles, climbed in and drove toward the marina where they'd find the yacht that would take them south to The Keys.

Once everyone was on board, the boat left the marina and headed out to open water.

Hunter and Savvie stood at the front rail for the first hour, only speaking when one or the other noticed something interesting along the shore or in the water. After a while, they settled inside the lounge area of the yacht. The other guys were either sleeping or playing cards—anything to pass the time.

Savvie leaned back and closed her eyes.

"Do you ever wonder how your life would've turned out if certain tragic events hadn't shaped your future?" she asked softly.

"I used to," he answered. "Then I realized it was a waste of time. I am who I am because of what happened. I like to think I became a better man than I was before."

Savvie snorted. "I don't know if I'm a better person for having killed my stepfather. Although, definitely a better shot."

"You care what happens to people who can't help themselves, or you wouldn't be on this yacht, headed into a situation we don't know enough about to predict the outcome. Maybe you're not necessarily a better person…"

"Gee, thanks."

He touched her hand. "Because you were a good person to begin with. You tried to save your mother from an abusive situation."

"And I failed," Savvie said. "She died anyway."

"You kept your stepfather from hurting others by taking him down."

She glanced up at him. "Killing someone doesn't make me a good person."

"Trying to protect someone who couldn't protect herself does. You're a better person than you give yourself credit for."

She didn't respond. Instead, she closed her eyes and pretended to sleep.

The last rays of sunlight melted into the ocean as they neared their destination. They tested the communications headsets and the radio they'd use to contact the yacht when they'd secured the captives. Last but not least, they applied dark camouflage paint to their faces and any exposed skin.

The captain stopped the yacht a couple of nautical miles short of their target. Far enough away that they couldn't see the island, and the people on the island couldn't see them.

The two teams loaded their Zodiacs with weapons and their pockets with ammo, C-4 explosives and a handful of detonators.

Hank handed Hunter a waterproof bag containing one of the two radios that would reach the yacht. "This bag also contains a satellite phone if all else fails. Contact Kyla. She knows to get word to our guys in the Colorado office. They're on standby in case things go south. If things get really bad, she'll send in the US Navy SEALs."

Starlight lit the heavens with a scattering of clouds occasionally blocking the light. They'd checked the weather less than an hour ago. A thin line of clouds was headed their way but wasn't expected to get to the island for a couple of hours. They needed to get in, find the captives and get back out before the line of showers made the seas too rough to navigate in Zodiacs filled with people.

They had no idea how many captives to expect or how to get them out without subduing every one of the guards the Caldwell mafia had employed.

They climbed aboard the Zodiacs and left the yacht, following the GPS devices loaded with the coordinates.

Stone, being the Navy SEAL, took the helm of the Team Yellowstone boat. Hunter sat beside Savvie on one side of the boat, salty spray peppering his skin as the craft bounced over low swells. Dax sat on Hunter's other side. Carter, Bubba and Moe sat on the opposite side. He hoped they weren't heading into a situation where they would be greatly outnumbered. His gut was knotted. They didn't know enough about the compound, how many armed men were guarding it, who was in charge or what he was capable of doing.

As the dark silhouette of the island came into view, the Zodiacs split, swinging wide of the entrance to the cove.

Stone headed for the beach on the southeast side of the little island. Starlight lit the way until they were within a hundred yards of shore. A cloud passed overhead, darkening the ocean. The white sand ahead was light enough they could see it and make their way toward it.

The cloud pushed past let the starlight shine brightly down on them.

They weren't alone.

Racing in from both sides were two motorboats skimming across the ocean's surface, moving faster than the Zodiac.

With nowhere else to go, Stone pushed their rubber boat as fast as it would go, heading for land.

Shots rang out over the roar of the engine.

Savvie and the team ducked low as the boat pushed forward.

"There are men on shore!" Dax called out.

Too late to change directions, and with boats coming at them from both sides, Stone sped toward the beach, encountering waves the closer they got.

"We're outnumbered," Savvie called out.

"They're shooting over our heads," Stone said.

"If they capture us, who will save the others?"

Savvie grabbed Hunter's arm. "While they fight, I'm going in."

He barely heard what she said before she flipped over backward into the water and disappeared.

Hunter's heart seized. He didn't think, didn't analyze, just reacted by tipping backward into a wave, his AR-15 slung crossways over his back.

When water rushed over him, he kicked hard. Once he came to the surface, he only had seconds to duck back under before one of the speed boats blasted over him, turning toward the shore.

The next time he surfaced, the Zodiac had skidded up onto the sandy shore, and his teammates bailed to either side and then lay low in the sand as bullets zipped over their heads.

Stone, Dax, Bubba, Carter and Moe low-crawled across the sand, keeping their heads down.

The speed boats weren't the kind of boats that could be easily beached. The drivers turned before they got too close to shore. The men on board fired toward Stone and the guys, completely oblivious to the fact that two of their team had bailed before the boat had gone ashore.

Hunter couldn't begin to help his team. Not when Savvie was out there in the water.

Where was Savvie? He spun, his chest tightening. Did she know how to swim? Had one of the speed boats hit her? Had she been pulled out to sea in a riptide or undertow? He couldn't call out and draw attention to himself and her.

Hunter tread water, making a three-hundred-sixty-degree turn, more desperate with each passing second. If she'd gone under and couldn't come up on her own, there was no way to find her in time. His heart sank into the pit of his belly.

No. Oh, hell no. Not again.

A face surfaced in front of him.

"Savvie," he cried and reached for her, pulling her to him and sending them both under.

He loosened his hold but didn't let go, kicking hard to bring them up for air. "Savvie," he gasped. "What the hell? You scared the shit out of me. Are you okay?"

She nodded.

"Don't ever do that to me again," he said, pressing his forehead to hers while still treading water.

"I'm sorry," she said, then raised a finger to her lips and pointed toward the shore.

The five men of his team were completely surrounded by more than a dozen men, each armed with an AR-15 rifle.

Hunter had to do something to help his friends. As he started for shore, a hand snagged his arm and arrested his movement.

Savvie held onto his arm.

He turned toward her. "They need help."

"The two of us won't make a difference," she

argued. "They'll still be outnumbered. This way, if they take them captive, they'll be inside the compound with the others."

"If they don't shoot them first," Hunter said.

The men surrounding the Yellowstone team closed in on them, yelling for them to drop their weapons.

Stone laid down his rifle and raised his hands. "Don't shoot."

Hunter and Savvie swam wide of the men on shore and the two motorboats circling close by. They headed for the far end of the beach, where a rocky outcropping stretched out into the ocean and the palm trees grew close to the water's edge.

All the while, Hunter watched his brothers in arms as they were herded into a line and marched off the beach, disappearing into the shadows of a stand of trees.

The speedboats raced away, leaving Hunter and Savvie in the clear to emerge from the water onto land.

"We need to follow them," Savvie said. "At a distance. They're probably following a path through the woods that goes to the compound."

They didn't have time to wring the water out of their clothes. His clothes and boots still damp from seawater, Hunter led the way, staying in the shadows of the trees until he reached the path his team had been herded down.

Moving quickly, he and Savvie closed the distance between them and the guards moving the team.

Hunter could hear the guards telling the guys to hurry along. When they came to a halt, Hunter could barely see them through the underbrush.

Someone shouted. Hunter couldn't make out the words. Then a loud clanking sound rang out.

The men ahead of Hunter and Savvie moved.

Hunter crept a little closer until he could make out the straight lines of the compound wall.

He shrank back into the shadows and watched as his friends disappeared through a heavy iron door.

Holy hell. How were he and Savvie going to get inside the fortress and rescue the prisoners they'd originally come for, and now, the men who were like family to him?

Hunter motioned for Savvie to move back into the jungle.

When he felt they were far enough away that they wouldn't be overheard, he tapped the mike on his radio headset.

He was surprised they were still in his ears, considering he'd been for a swim in the ocean with them. Yeah, they were still there, but would they work?

"Eagle Rock, this is Yellowstone. Come in."

Nothing. Not even static.

He tried again. "Eagle Rock, come in."

This time static filled his ear.

"Eagle Rock here," Hank's familiar voice filled Hunter's ear. A brief rush of relief filled him, followed by the crushing seriousness of their situation.

"Yellowstone, five of seven captured."

"Roger," Hank said. "Proceed as planned."

"Roger." Hunter wasn't sure how he and Savvie would breach the wall without the other guys to help. Hank and his team would go over from the other side of the compound.

He and Savvie wouldn't have his team to protect them or to have their backs. On the positive side, if he and Savvie could scale the wall, it might benefit them to move through the compound, just the two of them rather than a team of seven.

Staying far enough away from the compound wall and hiding in the shadows, Hunter and Savvie moved through the woods, studying the wall for a potential location to go over.

A cloud passed over the sky, making it too dark to see much of anything.

Hunter stopped and waited for the cloud to pass before continuing. When the stars shone down on the wall again, they illuminated several cracks in the surface, big enough for hand and footholds but higher than Hunter could reach by himself.

"Ever been rock climbing?" Savvie asked as if reading his mind.

"I have. You?" He glanced her way.

Her lips curled upward in a smile. "I have. I'd go first, but I know I can't help you from the top of the wall as much as I can help you down here." She tipped her chin toward the wall several yards from where they stood in the shadows. "I'll give you my knee and back to get you up as high as you can go. When you're on the wall, you can help me up."

"Deal," he nodded toward the wall. "On three?"

"One," Savvie said.

Hunter nodded. "Two."

Together they said, "Three," and then ran toward the wall.

Once they reached the base, Savvie bent, locked her fingers together and cupped her hands.

Hunter stepped into them, reached for the cracks, pulled himself up the wall and straddled the top, looking around for any guards that might be patrolling inside the compound perimeter. So far, the immediate vicinity remained clear.

When he was balanced, he leaned over as far as he could and extended his hand to Savvie.

She stood on her toes and could just clasp his hand with hers.

Hunter pulled her up to the top of the wall beside him and steadied her until she had her balance.

The building inside the compound next to them had no windows or doors on the side facing them.

Hunter pushed to his feet. The wall was wider than a balance beam, enough to walk along until they found an entry point into one of the structures or an alleyway between buildings.

Savvie stood beside Hunter.

"Drop to the ground, or follow the fence until we see an entry point?" Hunter whispered.

"Fence line," Savvie answered.

Hunter walked the top of the concrete wall until they passed the end of the structure, only to find another building past the first and a door tucked beneath an overhang.

"That's our entry point," Savvie said.

"What if it's locked?" he asked.

She grinned. "They taught us many useful skills in assassins' training. One of which was how to pick locks."

Hunter gripped her face in his hands and kissed her forehead. "You're amazing."

As quickly as he held her face in his hands, he released her and dropped quietly to the ground inside the compound.

He held up his arms.

Savvie lay atop the fence, then let her feet and legs drop over the side.

"Let go," Hunter said. "I've got you."

She slid down the fence into his arms.

He held her for a long moment, his body burning. Before he released her, he leaned close and whispered in her ear, "This is not the end, sweetheart. It's only the beginning."

"It might just be the end if we don't get moving." She turned in his arms and lifted her face to him. "Kiss me quick. We have a mission to finish."

His lips descended onto hers in a bone-melting crash that left him wanting so much more.

They had to get through this task before he could convince Savvie she could have a full, rich life after her career inflicting death.

He raised his head. "The sooner we succeed, the sooner we can focus on what we want next."

She opened her mouth to protest.

Hunter touched a finger to her lips. "We'll talk then."

He hoped this mission went smoothly and they all got back to Montana unscathed. Because they would talk, and he would make her see that she had other choices that didn't involve running. Choices that involved her staying close so that she could get to know him better.

Hunter already knew enough about Savvie to know they would be good together. He wanted the chance to prove it to her.

CHAPTER 13

EVERY TIME HUNTER KISSED HER, the walls around Savvie's heart crumbled a little more. If she wasn't careful, he'd completely demolish the walls she'd so carefully constructed after shooting her stepfather and joining the organization to become a highly trained and deadly effective assassin.

Hunter made her think she had a chance at a normal life. That kind of thinking was wrong and would only lead to heartache.

She squared her shoulders and focused on rescuing the Caldwell captives. She wasn't sure why this mission meant so much to her. If she'd refused the last assignment of taking Marcus Caldwell down, she'd never have known about the other people he'd lured into his lair only to be drugged and auctioned off like cattle at a sale barn.

She could have walked away before taking on that

assignment and would have been blissfully unaware and well on her way to a new life.

But then Marcus Caldwell would still be luring women into his sick world and sending them off to be trapped in the sex trade. The people he'd already captured would suffer that fate. And Savvie would never have met Hunter Falcon.

The man was everything a girl could want in a relationship. He was strong, capable of protecting her, appreciated her strengths and was an incredible lover.

Savvie had to believe she'd made the only choice she could have made. Perhaps Fate had given her the nudge to accept the assignment, and in doing so, sealed her fate.

She couldn't walk away from those who couldn't help themselves. It would be like losing her mother all over again. She'd waited too long to stop her stepfather. Someone had to stand up for the lost souls who'd given up on ever being rescued. She prayed she wasn't too late this time.

Savvie hurried toward the door on the side of the building, shrugged off the straps of her damp backpack and laid it on the ground beside the door. She reached inside and pulled out a small toolkit folded into a leather pouch. From the kit, she extracted a thin metal file and inserted it into the lock on the door handle. She fished around until she felt the locking mechanism trigger. She turned the knob, and the door opened.

Hunter stepped through while Savvie repacked her tools into her backpack, pulled her handgun out, tucked it into the waistband of her jeans and pulled her T-shirt over it.

Slipping the straps of the backpack over her shoulders, she followed Hunter into the building.

They hurried down a long hallway with doors on either side.

Hunter opened them, one by one, revealing a storage room with cleaning tools and supplies. The next was a large room filled with machines needed to run a compound as large as this. Air conditioning units, water heaters and generators, many of which were running, the sound deafening.

Hunter kept moving, carefully checking other doors and finding a laundry room and kitchen. He eased out of the doorway into the kitchen when they spied people moving around, preparing food.

The hallway ended in a T-junction. Left would take them toward the front of the complex. Right would take them to the rear.

Hunter chose to go to the right. Perhaps, like Savvie, he'd assumed the people in charge would be entertaining near the front of the establishment and keep the prisoners hidden in the back where their screams could not be heard.

They followed the hallway until it ended in a left

turn that led down a staircase into a lower level with concrete block walls and doors spaced at even intervals with windows into the rooms beyond.

Or cells. Each door was locked from the outside with a hasp and a keyed lock.

Hunter stopped at the first door and peered through the small window into the room beyond.

Savvie stepped up beside him and looked inside.

Curled into a fetal position on the concrete floor lay a young woman who couldn't be more than a teenager.

Hunter moved to the next door and peered through the window.

"We've found them," Savvie whispered.

Hunter touched the button on his headset. "Eagle Rock, Yellowstone."

"This is Eagle Rock, go ahead," Hank responded, his voice reassuring

"Art located,' Hunter reported. "Moving to rear of building."

"Any sign of Yellowstone three through nine?" Hank asked.

"No."

"Get them out," Hank said. "We'll take care of Yellowstone."

Savvie dropped the backpack, dug out the tools she needed and went to work on the first lock. It took a couple of minutes to make the lock open.

Hunter motioned to the next.

Savvie worked on the next lock while Hunter removed the lock from the hasp and entered the first room where the teenage girl had pushed to her feet.

He held a finger to his lips and urged the girl to leave the cell and wait while they freed the others.

One by one, Savvie unlocked the padlocks. She was only halfway down the line of cells when one of the freed women whimpered and stumbled back into her cell, pulling the door closed. Others did the same until the hallway was clear but for Hunter and Savvie.

Footsteps sounded from around the corner at the end of the line of cells.

Savvie and Hunter ducked into one of the empty cells and pulled the door closed with a soft snick.

A big, burly man rounded the corner with a bandage wrapped around his bicep, followed by another man with a big knot on his forehead.

Savvie had seen these men before in the Setai Hotel in Marcus's penthouse suite.

Savvie dropped to the floor and lay on her side in a fetal position like the first woman they'd encountered.

Hunter pressed his back to the wall beside the door.

The man with the bandaged bicep peered through the window into the room where Savvie lay on her side, looking back at the man through the veil of her eyelashes.

Burly man's eyes narrowed. He shook his head and moved to the next door that she hadn't yet unlocked.

A key scraped on metal and was followed by the click of a lock disengaging.

A woman's moaning protest sounded as the men dragged the person from the next cell.

Savvie leaped to her feet.

When the two men passed the cell where she and Hunter hid, she held her breath and waited.

Once the two men were past the door to their cell, Savvie and Hunter eased the cell door open. Despite their care, the hinge let out a loud squeak.

The men turned as one.

Hunter and Savvie didn't give them a fighting chance. They attacked first.

Savvie took the man she'd stabbed before in the bicep, dropped him to the ground and jacked his arm up between his shoulder blades.

Hunter slammed the other man against the wall. The guy hit the floor and lay still. Hunter grabbed his arms and dragged him into a cell. He came back out, holding up a set of keys, and then tossed them to her before dragging the burly guy into the same cell, When he came back out, he snapped one of the locks they'd removed into place.

Once they had all the young women out of their cells, they half-walked, half-ran with them back toward the machine room and the door they'd entered through minutes before.

Between Savvie and Hunter, they got the women over the wall, one by one.

Once the last one went over, Hunter helped Savvie up onto the wall. Together, they slid down the other side.

The crunch of footsteps on gravel had Hunter and Savvie taking up fighting stances, weapons ready.

As the two men came into view, they held up their hands.

The one in the lead whispered, "Yellowstone, we're Eagle Rock. Boomer and Taz. Hank sent us to help get the ladies out of here. Our Zodiac wasn't compromised."

Hunter nodded. "Good. Then you don't need me. I'm going back in to help find the rest of our guys."

"I'm going, too." Savvie hurried after Hunter, gave him the boost he needed to scale the wall and waited for him to reach down for her.

When he didn't, she frowned. "What are you doing?" She reached up at high as she could. "I'm going with you."

"Go with the women," Hunter said. "Make sure they get out. I'll see you later."

"This is bullshit," she whispered. "I'm going with you."

He disappeared, dropping to the ground on the other side.

ELLE JAMES

"No," she whispered, her heart breaking into a million pieces. "Don't leave me." She looked around for help to scale the wall.

Boomer and Taz had rounded up the women and were moving them into the woods for the trek back to their Zodiac.

For a moment, Savvie stared at the wall, defeated. Starlight shone on the wall, casting little shadows on the chinks in the concrete blocks. If she could just get to the first one...

Savvie backed up several yards. Then she sprinted at the wall. When she got close enough, she leaped as high as she could and touched her shoe against the bricks, pushing herself higher and reaching for the crack in the brick.

Her fingers curled into the bricks, the treads on her tennis shoes gripping the coarse surface.

When gravity brought the weight of her body down, she almost lost her hold.

"No way," she said through gritted teeth. "You will not leave me behind." Shifting her fingers, she got a better grip and reached for the next crack, then placed her foot in another flaw in the wall. Working her way slowly upward, she pulled herself onto the top of the wall and slid over the other side, dropping lightly to the ground.

Then she was running toward the door she'd opened by picking the lock.

Once inside the building, she looked for Hunter. He wasn't in the hallway with the mechanical room.

Savvie ran to the T-junction. To the right were the cells where the Caldwells had kept the women they'd offer up for sale to the highest bidders.

Savvie turned left, heading toward the front of the building and, hopefully, toward Hunter.

She'd gotten them into this mission to rescue those women. If anything happened to any of the Brotherhood Protectors, it would be her fault for dragging them into this effort.

She'd promised Kyla she'd make sure Stone returned home in one piece. If anything happened to him, their baby would grow up without a father. Or with a stepfather who could never love her and would abuse her and her mother.

No. No. No.

And then there were her growing feelings for Hunter. If anything happened to him, she would never know what he wanted to talk about. What he meant by it wasn't over between them. She'd never know if they could fall in love and make a life for themselves despite her past career choice.

Damn it!

Where was he?

Savvie ran to the next T-junction in the hallway, slowed and peered carefully around the corner.

The hallway was empty. Voices sounded to the left, moving toward her.

Savvie turned right and raced down the corridor, slowing long enough to twist doorknobs. Most of these doors were locked. If she didn't find an open one soon, the men belonging to the voices would see her. She'd be captured, adding one more worry to the men who'd already helped her out of a bad situation in Miami.

Nearing the end of the hallway, she was running out of options. The last door she tried opened. Knowing she only had seconds to decide, she pushed through the door and gently closed it behind her.

Footsteps sounded, coming closer.

Savvie glanced around the interior of the room, searching for a place to hide.

She was in a sitting room with an ornate mahogany desk taking up the other side of the room with a laptop open on its surface.

With no other hiding place, she ducked behind the desk and folded her body into the knee space, making her five-foot-seven-inch frame as small as possible.

She'd barely settled when the door to the room banged open.

"How could you let this happen?" a man said. "You promised to remove the obstacles. There's been nothing but obstacles since my brother's death."

Instantly, Savvie realized that Marcus's brother, Jesse Caldwell, was in charge and the one behind the sex trafficking operation.

"Especially that woman you sent to get Marcus out of the picture," he continued. "You were supposed to take care of her as well."

"I can't help the men you hire are incompetent."

"You should've known they couldn't contain her. She's a fucking trained assassin. One of yours."

Savvie's blood ran hot through her veins, anger blossoming like a pervasive flower with a heady scent.

She'd been set up by her handler in the organization.

Bastard!

She fought the urge to leap out from beneath the desk and confront him.

Footsteps crossed the room, moving toward the desk.

"Well, Don, your mistake will cost you," Jesse said. "I'm docking ten thousand from what we agreed on."

"The hell you are," Don said, his tone tight and angry.

"You only accomplished half of the task. You were supposed to take care of Marcus and then eliminate her. But you didn't, did you?" Jesse demanded. "Your precious assassin is now making it her mission to destroy my operation."

The more she listened, the angrier she got.

A telephone rang on the desk.

Jesse Caldwell stepped behind the desk and lifted a phone off the receiver. "What now? You're fucking kidding me. Well, don't just stand around with your thumbs up your ass—find them. The auction is in full swing. We have to deliver what they're bidding on!" He slammed down the phone. "This is a fucking disaster. Neither of us is getting paid if we don't find those women."

"Did your men let the guys they caught on the beach get away?" Don asked. "Did they take the women?"

Savvie's anger took a back burner. What had they done with Hunter's team?

"No," Jesse said. "I had them drop them in the tank. It's secure. The only way out is to drop them a line. That isn't going to happen."

"What's the tank?" Don asked.

"A natural blow hole off the southeast corner of the compound. It fills with water at high tide and traps whatever falls in there until the tide recedes hours later. The tide is coming in now. It won't be long."

Savvie's heart squeezed hard. Hunter's team would drown at high tide if they didn't get them out soon.

She willed the men to leave, praying she'd have enough time to get to the tank and drop a line for the men so they could climb out.

"I don't like that those men found this location," Don said.

"They wouldn't have found us if you'd gotten rid

of your assassin. I'm surprised she wasn't with them. Are you sure they got everyone from that boat?"

"That's what they said." Jesse tapped on keys. "In the meantime, we need to move money from the Cayman accounts to the Swiss accounts. They found us here. They might find our accounts." More keyboard typing sounded above Savvie's head.

"Okay, done," Jess said. "We need to get back to the conference room and check on the progress of the auction."

"Auction progress won't matter if they don't find the ladies," Don reminded him.

"It's a small island," Jess assured him. "They'll find them."

After the two men left the room, Savvie scrambled out from beneath the desk and ran for the door.

She had to find the tank before it filled with water.

CHAPTER 14

When Hunter raced back into the compound, he'd skipped the building they'd entered before and moved to the next. The smaller structure proved to be a storage shed for tools, machines and a tractor. There were no secret attics or trap doors. His team wasn't in the shed.

The next building was larger, a long low building with windows running its length. He peered through one of the windows into what appeared to be some kind of open-bay barracks.

He moved on, his gut telling him he was running out of time.

As he rounded a corner of the last building, he spotted a line of men shining flashlights into the shadows, moving through the compound, probably looking for the missing women.

Out of the corner of his eyes, a shadowy figure captured Hunter's attention.

Hank Patterson eased up to him. "I thought you'd be with the women getting them to the Zodiacs."

Hunter shook his head. "Not leaving this island without my team," he said. "I take it you haven't located them?

Hank shook his head. "Not yet. We've been through all the buildings. No sign of them whatsoever."

Hank nodded toward the men searching the grounds. "Are they looking for the women?"

"That's my assumption," Hunter said. "Can't sell what you don't have. It's ironic they're searching for the women we found, and we're looking for my team they found."

"They're leaving the compound," Hank said. "I hope they don't get to the Zodiacs before the ladies. Did Savvie go with them?"

Hunter nodded. "She wanted to come with me, but I told her she needed to see the ladies made it off the island."

Hank snorted softly. "How'd she take being told what to do?"

"She wasn't happy."

The compound's heavy iron doors remained open while the men searched the grounds near the wall.

"Do you think they could have taken my guys somewhere outside the walls?" Hunter asked.

Hank's brow wrinkled. "It's possible."

A slim, shadowy figure approached the iron doors, stopped and peered out.

Hunter leaned forward. "Do you see that?"

Hank nodded. "Too slim to be a guy."

Hunter's pulse kicked up as he recognized the way the figure moved. "Holy shit."

"What?" Hank asked.

"It's not a guy," Hunter said. "It's Savvie."

"Go," Hank said. "I'll rally my guys and follow."

Hunter left the corner of the building where he'd been crouched in the dark, watching the men searching the compound.

He moved quickly, trying to stick to the shadows as best he could, finally having to cross an open area with starlight shining down on him.

Once through the iron doors, he avoided the line of men searching the edge of the woods and the road leading toward the cove.

Hunter paused in the shadow of a palm and searched the underbrush for Savvie's slim silhouette.

He looked in the opposite direction from where the men were heading toward the cove.

A movement caught his eye, heading toward the southeast corner of the compound.

But it wasn't the slim, dark silhouette of Savvie. This figure was taller with a barrel chest, moving with less grace than Savvie.

Where had Savvie gone? And who was this moving outside the wall?

Hunter suspected whoever it was could be following Savvie.

He followed, closing in on the man while placing his feet carefully to avoid making noise.

The ground was rockier, leading out to a point in the water with cover and concealment diminishing quickly.

The closer he got to the rocky outcropping, the louder the waves thundered.

Ahead of the man, a dark figure picked its way across the rocks.

Savvie.

She seemed to be looking for something, zigzagging across the rocky surface until she came to a stop and bent over.

Hunter wasn't sure, but he thought he heard her call out.

The man between Hunter and Savvie increased his speed, barreling toward her.

"Savvie!" Hunter yelled and ran toward her. He couldn't shoot the man because Savvie was in the line of fire. It was too risky. His bullet might hit her instead.

Savvie didn't look up. The waves crashing against the rocks must have drowned out his call.

The man with the barrel chest was within two yards of Savvie, and he wasn't slowing down.

Hunter ran all out, racing to get to Savvie. "Savvie!" he yelled again.

She spun but not soon enough to dodge the man.

He plowed into her like a linebacker, knocking her backward. Instead of falling onto the rocks, she disappeared completely.

Hunter's heart flipped.

The man who'd hit her bent over, staring downward.

As Hunter neared him, the man turned and aimed a pistol at Hunter's chest.

"One step closer, and I'll shoot you," the man said.

"Then you better shoot me because if you hurt Savvie, I'm going to kill you."

The man fired his weapon, his hand shaking so badly, the bullet went wide, missing his target.

Anger boiled inside Hunter. He stalked the guy, stopping just three feet short of the man.

Beyond where he stood was a hole the size of a bus. The waves making the crashing sounds on the rocky shore made softer sounds moving in and out of the cave below.

Hunter couldn't see to the bottom of the hole to know whether Savvie was all right. If he wanted to get there, he had to go through the man with the gun.

"Move," he demanded.

"No," the man shook his head.

Hunter didn't have time to waste on this piece of

shit. He swung a sidekick hard and fast, catching the man's gun wrist and knocking the pistol out of his grip. It skittered across a rock and slipped between crevices.

The man clutched his wrist, roared and plowed into Hunter, knocking him backward.

Hunter staggered several steps before he regained his footing and slung the man away from him. He had to get to that hole. If Savvie was down there, she could be hurt.

He'd only taken a few steps backward when the man hit him in the gut almost knocking him into the hole. Hunter grabbed the man's shirt, rolled onto his back, and flipped the guy over his head. The man landed on the rim of the hole, scrambled for a moment and then slid inside.

"Help!" a voice called from below.

"Help!" another voice yelled.

Hunter peered over the edge into the darkness.

"Hunter!" Stone's voice called out. "Throw us a rope! Hurry! The water's up to our waists, and the current is dragging us out."

Hunter searched the area around him, the starlight half-hidden behind clouds. He pulled his cell phone from his pocket, hit the flashlight function and shined it all around. When he didn't find a rope, he expanded his search.

"Hurry!" Stone called out.

Several yards away, he saw a frayed rope hidden

behind a large stone. The rope had knots at regular intervals along its length.

Hunter tied the end of the rope to a huge boulder and dropped the length into the swirly hole.

"Sending Savvie up first. Help her get there," Stone yelled from below.

Savvie started up the rope. Soon, Hunter could see the top of her head. He grabbed the rope and hauled her the rest of the way to the top, grabbed her wrist and dragged her onto the stone ledge.

She turned immediately and flung the rope down for the others.

Dax came up next, scaling the rope as fast as he could.

Right behind him was Bubba, then Carter and Moe.

"It's bad down there," Moe said. "I almost didn't make it out."

Hunter touched the rope. It was pulled tight and jerking as if someone was climbing it. "Stone's on the rope."

"Help him," Savvie cried, grabbing the end.

The others all grabbed a section and pulled, leaning back.

When Stone's head rose above the rocky ledge, a cheer went up. They didn't let up on their hold until their leader was safely out.

"What about the guy who pushed Savvie in?" Hunter asked.

"Swept out to sea," Stone said. "I tried to hold onto him, but he must have hit his head going down.

"Move back," Savvie cried. "It's going to blow!"

Savvie and the men backed away, giving the blow hole enough distance that when the waves pushed in below, the water that shot up like a geyser only got a little spray on them.

Hunter pulled Savvie into his arms and held her close. She wrapped her arms around his waist and hugged him back.

"We need to get out of here," Stone said.

They left the rocky point and slipped into the shadows of the trees, moving toward the beach where they'd left the Zodiac.

"Yellowstone, this is Eagle Rock," Hank's voice came through Hunter's headset.

"This is Yellowstone," Hunter responded.

"Sorry we didn't get to you in time. Ran into trouble. Status of your team?"

"Intact and heading for the beach," Hunter said.

"Our ride moved in to pick up our passengers," Hank said. "It won't take you long to reach it once you're on the water. See you aboard."

They made it to the beach without meeting any more resistance, and thankfully, the Zodiac was where they'd left it, unharmed.

They pushed it out into the surf, climbed aboard and left the little island.

Hunter wrapped his arm around Savvie and held

her close all the way back to the yacht, where they reunited with Hank's guys and the survivors they'd rescued from the Caldwell mafia.

"We're headed for Key West," Hank said. "The Coast Guard will meet us there, and we'll transfer the ladies into their care."

Savvie, Hunter and the rest of the Brotherhood Protectors spent the remainder of the trip helping the women who were still under the lingering effects of the drugs they'd been given and the trauma of being kidnapped.

By the time they met up with the Coast Guard, the team was given the option of driving back to Miami or remaining with the yacht to make the trip by sea.

They all opted for returning by sea.

The sun came up as soon as they left Key West and warmed the air around them.

Hunter and Savvie claimed lounge chairs on the deck and napped part of the time.

The captain's crew served them breakfast with mimosas.

By the time they pulled into the dock in Miami, they were ready to be home but still had the long flight back to Montana.

Hunter dozed off several times but woke up looking for Savvie. It would take time to get over the nightmare of seeing her pushed into the blowhole.

Almost losing her made him that much more

determined to convince her to stay. He'd have to up his game and show her he was willing to be with her no matter the risk.

WHEN THEY LANDED IN BOZEMAN, they still had a two-hour drive to West Yellowstone. No one spoke on the drive down; everyone was exhausted and ready for a shower and food.

As they rolled up to the lodge, Kyla was the first person out the door.

Stone caught her in his arms and hugged her as tightly as he could with her big belly in the way. "See? I got back in plenty of time to be here for the baby."

"You only did that because you knew I'd come looking for you if you didn't." She winked up at him and shot a glance toward Savvie, mouthing the words, *Thank you.*

Everyone scattered to get showers, promising to meet up for the dinner Cookie had prepared.

Hunter walked with Savvie up the stairs and paused in front of her door long enough to take her into his arms and kiss her thoroughly.

She inserted her key in the door and pushed it open.

"See you after a shower," he said.

"I'd rather see you in the shower." She grabbed his shirt front and tugged him through the door.

Hunter didn't argue when he wanted it as much as she did.

They left a trail of clothing through her room and into the bathroom, where they stepped beneath the warm water and washed the salt from each other's bodies, exploring every inch of skin in the process.

His cock was hard and ready, but protection was a room away.

"We can go to your room," she offered.

"Or we can have dinner because your stomach is growling and pick up where we left off later." He kissed her long and hard.

They dried each other off, and Hunter wrapped a towel around his waist and left to return to his own room to dress.

They met up in the hallway a few minutes later.

Savvie wore a light blue floral dress and strappy sandals. She'd brushed her damp hair back from her face.

"You're more beautiful every time I see you." He kissed her and held out his arm.

"You're not so bad yourself," she said.

At the big table in the dining room, everyone was there, including everyone's significant others.

Stone filled them in on a conversation he'd had with Hank.

"Before Hank's team left the island, a helicopter landed, apparently to pick up Jesse Caldwell. While the pilot took a bathroom break, Hank's guys disabled the helicopter. They also disabled the boats in the cove, leaving no way for Jesse Caldwell or his 'guests' to leave the island before the feds could get there. They're all in custody now. With the testimonies from all the women we rescued, Caldwell should spend plenty of time in prison."

"What about Don, my handler from the organization?" Savvie asked.

"Hank said they recovered his body," Stone replied. "He won't be colluding with human traffickers ever again."

"Now, Savvie," Kyla gave her a pointed look, "about retired life. You really should consider Montana. More specifically, West Yellowstone. There's not as much traffic as on the east coast, cleaner air—when there aren't wildfires—and less crime. Plus, you'll be closer to me."

Savvie laughed. "That's quite the sales pitch."

Bubba's sweetheart, Chelsea, set down her fork. "Yellowstone National Park is so close, there's so much wildlife to witness and the fishing is phenomenal."

"Someone did promise to take me fishing." Savvie cocked an eyebrow in Hunter's direction.

"I'm ready whenever you are," Hunter said. "How's tomorrow? We can take a lunch and make a day of it."

"Sounds lovely," Savvie smiled. "As long as I can

fish from shore. I'm not ready to go under again anytime soon."

"Ha!" Stone grinned. "Me, either." His grin turned serious. "Thanks for coming to find us in the blow hole."

"You would have done it for me," Savvie said.

"Because that's what we do for each other," Stone said.

"And other people," Bubba added.

"You could come to work for the Brotherhood Protectors," Stone suggested.

Hunter's heart leaped. "Yeah, we need more females." And it would mean he could see her more. They'd have time to get to know each other.

"You're not concerned by my previous profession?" Savvie asked. "Or that I killed a man when I was seventeen years old?"

"No," Stone said. "And Hank's on board as well."

"I'll think about it," Savvie said.

"Take your time," Stone said. "The offer's open."

Dinner concluded, and everyone stepped out on the back porch to enjoy the sunset and cool evening breeze.

"Want to go for a walk?" Hunter asked Savvie.

"Yes, please," she said and hooked her hand around his elbow.

They set off down the road.

"I hope you decide to stay in West Yellowstone," Hunter said. "No matter what job you decide on."

"Why?" she asked.

"Because I like you," he said. "I think I'm well on my way to loving you if I'm not already there. When that asshole pushed you into the blow hole…" He shook his head. "I don't know what the future holds for us, and I promise not to rush you, but I'd like to date you so you can see how much we have in common and so I can convince you to love me, too."

She stopped and turned to look him in the eye. "What if someone comes looking for revenge?"

"I'm not afraid for myself—and I'll have your back."

She laid her hand against his chest. "I fully intended on leaving once we got back from Miami, but now…"

He smiled and cupped the back of her neck. "Now, you're already in love with me. I mean, what's not to love?"

She laughed. "I'm finding that out. And I don't want to leave. Your team is family, and I'd really like to belong to a family. The kind of family that looks out for each other."

"That's what we do." He raised her hand to his lips. "So, are you staying?"

She drew in a deep breath and let it out slowly, her lips curling up. "Yes, please."

He wrapped his arms around her and swung her in a circle. "Before you know it, you'll love me as much as I love you."

She laughed. "I already do."

EPILOGUE

One month later...

"So, I hear you and Hunter are house hunting. Has he asked you to marry him yet?" Kyla asked from where she sat at her computer desk.

"Yes, we're looking for a place to live. No, he hasn't asked me to marry him." Savvie frowned at Kyla. "Shouldn't you be in a lounge chair with your feet up?"

"I'm only here for a couple of minutes. My back hurts too much to sit at a computer for too long. I'll be glad when baby Jacobs gets here, and I can have my body back." She rubbed a hand over her belly. "Not that I mind being pregnant, but nine months has come and gone. It's time."

"Wasn't your due date three days ago?" Savvie asked.

"Yes. My doctor said she'll induce at a week over. I hope I don't go that long." She pushed away from the computer and smiled at Savvie. "Today would be a good day to have a baby, don't you think?"

"Absolutely." Savvie grinned. "Maybe it's all a mindset."

"Mindset? Ha!" Kyla looked down at her belly. "This child has a mind of its own." She held onto the table as she stood, a frown ceasing her brow. "My back really is hurting. I think I'll go lay down."

"Hello, ladies." Hunter entered the war room carrying a bouquet of flowers. He leaned down and pressed a kiss to Savvie's forehead. "How's work going? Brotherhood Protectors keeping you busy?"

"Kyla's showing me what she does for the team so I can take over while she's on maternity leave," Savvie said. "Which should be soon."

Hunter shot a smile at the pregnant woman. "Is Kyla trying to convince you to have a baby, or is she scaring you out of it altogether?"

"Both." Savvie laughed.

Kyla's lips twisted. "Glad I could help." She pinned Hunter with a pointed glance. "You going to ask Savvie to marry you anytime soon?"

"I'm giving her time to know for sure I'm her one and only. When she's absolutely sure, I'll ask." He winked at Savvie.

Kyla cocked an eyebrow in Savvie's direction. "Is Hunter your one and only? Do you love him more than chocolate?"

Savvie nodded. "I do."

Kyla turned to Hunter. "Then what are you waiting for?"

"That's all I needed to know." He reached into his pocket and pulled out a small box. When he dropped to one knee, Savvie's heart skipped several beats then sped to catch up.

"Savvie Sanders, I think you are the most beautiful woman inside and out, and I would be the happiest man alive if you'd agree to marry me."

Savvie dropped to her knees, gathered his hands in hers, ring box and all, and pressed them to her heart. "Hunter, you're the best thing that ever happened to me. Yes, I will marry you. The sooner the better, so we can get on with our lives together."

Kyla pressed a hand to her back and to her belly. "Now that you've settled your engagement, could someone call Stone and let him know that you're taking me to the hospital? It's go time!"

SAVING JENNA

BROTHERHOOD PROTECTORS
YELLOWSTONE BOOK #7

New York Times & USA Today
Bestselling Author

ELLE JAMES

YELLOWSTONE

SAVING JENNA

BROTHERHOOD PROTECTORS

New York Times & USA Today Bestselling Author

ELLE JAMES

CHAPTER 1

After checking in at the nurses' station on the third floor, Jenna Jenkins hurried to the room number she'd been given. She knocked lightly on the door.

"Jenna?" a soft, familiar voice called out.

Jenna pushed through the swinging door and entered the room. The lights were muted, but there was no mistaking the face of the woman lying against the stark white sheets, her ginger hair fanned out on the pillow behind her.

"Brittany, sweetie." Jenna rushed to her bedside and wrapped her arms around her younger half-sister as best she could without disturbing the IV attached to her arm.

"Oh, Jenna," Brittany clung to her, her arms thinner than the last time she'd seen her almost a year ago.

A lump rose in Jenna's throat. She swallowed hard. "Oh, baby, what happened? Why are you here?" She leaned back. "Are you hurt? Sick? Tell me. What's going on? When did you get in town?"

Her sister gave her a weak smile. "A couple of weeks ago."

Jenna frowned. "You've been in Bozeman for a couple of weeks?" She shook her head. "Why didn't you let me know?"

Her sister shrugged. "You have your own life." She glanced down at the IV in her arm. "I didn't want to bother you with mine."

Jenna's heart squeezed hard in her chest. "You're never a bother, Brittany. Never. I love you."

A tear rolled down her cheek. Brittany brushed it away. "Yeah, well, I love you, too. And that's why I didn't want to bother you with the mess I've made of my life. I'm twenty-six years old. I should've figured things out by now." She waved a hand around the room. "Instead, I dropped out of college and have bounced around from one dead-end job to another." Her voice faded. "And one worthless boyfriend to another."

Jenna touched a finger to Brittany's chin and raised her head until she was forced to look at her. "You're still my sister. No matter what. You can always come to me. You always have a place to go. I told you that a long time ago."

Another tear rolled down her cheek. "I know. But

you're so...so...together. You have your degree, a great job with the FBI and a guy who makes you happy."

Jenna snorted. "I'm not as together as you think. Ryan and I broke up almost a year ago."

Brittany's brow creased. "Oh, Jenna, I'm so sorry."

"It's okay. We dated for five years, and he never made a move to make it permanent. I finally told him to shit or get off the pot."

Brittany's eyes widened. "You didn't."

Jenna nodded. "I did. And he got off the pot. He's since met his soulmate, married and is already expecting a baby. He's happily married. I'm happily single. It's all good." Though she made light of it, Ryan's quick rebound after breaking up with her had hurt more than she'd admit.

She still wondered what was wrong with her that he hadn't been able to commit to her after five years but could commit to the new girlfriend after only a few months...?

"But look at you," Brittany said. "You've still got it together."

"What other choice do I have?" Jenna sighed. "Life goes on."

Brittany nodded. "Yes, it does."

Jenna tipped her head toward the IV. "So, what brings you to the hospital? Kidney stones? Ruptured appendix?" She prayed it wasn't anything more serious like the leukemia that had claimed their mother. She held her breath, waiting for Brittany's answer.

Her sister glanced away. "I made a mistake moving in with Larry."

Based on her sister's judgment in men, Jenna wasn't surprised. Now wasn't the time to say that. "How so?"

"He wasn't who I thought he was."

"I thought you said he was a pharmaceutical salesman."

Brittany met Jenna's gaze. "Oh, he is that, but I thought I was his one and only." She snorted and looked down at her hands. "I found out those long stretches where he was away weren't just to make sales. He was going home to Salt Lake City to his wife and kids."

Jenna's jaw hardened. "That bastard." As more tears flowed down Brittany's cheeks, Jenna took her hand. "At least you found out before it went too far."

Brittany's fingers curled around hers. "That's just it…" She met Jenna's gaze. "Things went too far."

Jenna's brow dipped. "What do you mean?"

The swinging door pushed inward as a nurse backed in, pulling a cart through. She wore her hair in a thick braid twisted into a tight knot at her nape and covered with a hair net. "Miss Berry, it's dinner time," she announced.

"That's Nurse Grey," Brittany said.

Jenna cast a brief glance at the older nurse and

returned her attention to Brittany. "Your dinner can wait a moment. What do you mean *things went too far?*"

Brittany's lips quirked on the corners. "My dinner can wait, but hers can't." She nodded toward the woman entering the room as she slowly spun the cart to reveal a clear plastic container.

A soft mewling sound grew louder. Movement inside the container made Jenna's breath catch in her throat. She straightened and turned fully to look into what she now recognized as a hospital bassinet. Inside lay a tiny baby cocooned in a tightly wrapped blanket, its face turning dark pink as it revved up the volume from mewling to full-on crying.

Jenna looked from the crying baby to her sister. "I don't understand."

Brittany laughed. "It's a baby. Jenna," her sister paused, "meet your niece."

The nurse gathered the baby from the bassinet and carried it to Brittany, placing the infant in her mother's arms.

Mother.

"You're a mother?" Jenna struggled to process this information, though the evidence was as clear as the baby in her sister's arms. "But how?"

Brittany's lips twisted. "Really?" She adjusted her hospital gown, exposing a full breast. The nurse helped her adjust the baby's position, pressing her face to the distended nipple.

243

At first, the infant didn't seem to know what to do, but then its little lips latched on.

Brittany sucked in a sharp breath.

"It might hurt at first, but before long, you'll get used to it," the nurse reassured her with a smile. "And mother's milk is best for your little one." She straightened. "I'll be back in a few minutes to check on you."

"Thank you," Brittany said.

When Nurse Grey left the room, Brittany fussed with the baby. "She hasn't quite got the hang of this yet." Finally, she looked up, her brow furrowing. "Aren't you going to say something?"

"Why didn't you tell me you were pregnant?"

"Things were on-again-off-again with Larry. We had our fights and made up so many times. I thought it was normal and that I was handling it without help from my big sister. We were pregnant. A baby would make it all work." She lifted a shoulder and let it fall. "Until I found out he was married."

Jenna shook her head. "Every time we talked…"

"I know. I should've told you then. But the timing never seemed right. It seems like every time I think I get things right, they fall apart. I wanted to handle this on my own."

"But this isn't a rent payment or a new set of tires." Jenna waved a hand toward the bundle in her sister's arms. "It's a baby. A lifetime commitment."

Brittany's brow dipped lower. "I know. I should've told you, but it's complicated."

Afraid to ask, she did anyway. "How complicated?"

Brittany bit her bottom lip. "When I confronted Larry about the fact he was married, I asked him if he was going to leave his wife and kids." She snorted. "He said no. I asked him if he planned on helping me support our child. He said no. When I asked how he expected me to support the baby, he said he expected me to give it up for adoption."

"Bastard," Jenna whispered between clenched teeth.

Brittany stared down at the baby girl in her arms. "After he drank a six-pack of beer, he passed out watching a football game. I packed my bag with what little I owned, took some money from Larry's wallet and walked out. I drove to the one place I had any family…Bozeman. You were my backup plan."

"You didn't call me."

"I couldn't," Brittany whispered. "You've bailed me out too many times already. I had to figure out this mess on my own." She sighed. "Only I think I made it worse."

Jenna dropped into a chair beside the bed, unsure she could handle more of Brittany's drama.

Her sister continued. "I took a temporary job as a bartender only because the guy who owned the bar also rented me a garage apartment. He knew I didn't have much money and that it wouldn't go far. On top of that, my car quit working. He felt sorry for me and let me work a few hours a day. It wasn't much, but the tips helped."

Jenna thought back over the past couple of weeks. How long had it been since she'd talked with her sister? She usually called every other week. Had it been longer? What kind of older sister was she if she didn't check on her sister more often than once a month?

Brittany shifted the baby to the other breast and helped her latch on before continuing. "Anyway, I realized that working at a bar and living in a tiny garage apartment that was smaller than a college dorm room wasn't going to cut it. But I couldn't afford anything else. I was feeling desperate. The baby was almost here, and I couldn't support it."

Jenna started to say something.

Brittany held up a hand. "I know I should've called you., but I didn't. My mistake. I was working at the bar when a man came in and sat at the bar. He asked for a rum and coke. While I fixed it for him, he asked me when my baby was due. We talked for a while. He seemed nice. I confided that I was thinking of giving up my baby for adoption, so it could have a better life than I could provide."

Jenna's heart sank. "What did you do?"

Brittany stared at her sister, her eyes filling with tears. "He told me he and his wife had tried to have children, but after five miscarriages and one live birth that ended in the baby dying from SIDs, they'd given up. They lived in a big empty house. He made plenty of money to raise a dozen children and send them all to college without taking out a loan."

"Money isn't everything," Jenna said.

"That's easy to say when you have it," Brittany said. "But it wasn't just the money. He said he loved his wife so much and wished he could give her the baby they both wanted so badly. They were exactly what my baby needed to make it in life. A happily married couple able to give my baby the life I couldn't."

Jenna knew where this was going, her heart sinking into the pit of her belly. "You told him he could adopt your baby?" Her gaze rested on the sweet baby girl pressed against her mother's breast.

"I made him give me a copy of his driver's license and a copy of his savings and investments statement. My boss at the bar had a cop buddy run a background check on the guy. He was a legit, upstanding citizen in the community with no criminal record. His wife was a volunteer at the local food bank. I drove by the address he gave me, the same one on his driver's license. It was a big, beautiful house with a huge yard. I couldn't give my baby any of that."

Jenna would have helped, but she held her tongue and let her sister continue.

"I agreed to let him adopt my baby, knowing it

would be the best life for it. I was fully prepared to hand it over." She stared down at the baby, suckling at her breast. "Until she finally made her appearance." Brittany's lips curled into a soft smile. "Once I held her in my arms, I knew I'd do anything to make her happy. Anything but give her up." Brittany looked up and caught Jenna's gaze. "He paid a lot of money to help with my expenses when I couldn't work the last couple of weeks. I owe him a lot." She shook her head. "But I can't give him my baby."

Jenna pressed a hand to her tight chest, thankful she'd gotten to her sister before the man showed up demanding the baby he'd bought and paid for. "We'll pay him back."

"I have no money," Brittany said.

"I do," Jenna offered. "I put back some money for a rainy day." At that moment, no rainstorm was as important as keeping Brittany and her baby girl together. "We'll figure it out." She patted her sister's arm. "Together."

Tears slid down Brittany's face. "I really tried not to rely on you. I want to be able to take care of myself and my child. I just can't right now."

"That's what family is for," Jenna said. "We take care of each other." She wrapped her arms around her sister and the baby and hugged them gently, tears slipping down her own cheeks. "And no more secrets. We have to work together to make a good home for the baby." She gave a short laugh. "Does she have a name?"

Brittany shook her head. "I didn't want to give her one if I was going to give her up for adoption. Now... I don't know."

"I always liked the name Olivia," Jenna offered.

"I like it," Brittany glanced down at the baby with a light orange fuzz across her scalp. "I've always thought Brenna or Blakely were good names."

"Blakely." Jenna nodded. "I like it." She looked down at the baby and smiled. "It's a good name for a little spitfire like her mother." She gently feathered her fingers over the baby's fuzzy scalp, her heart already swelling with love for her niece.

"Blakely Berry," Brittany rolled the name on her tongue. "I think we have a name. Don't you, sweet-heart?" she spoke softly.

The nurse returned. "Do you need help with the baby?"

Brittany shook her head and smiled at Jenna. "I have my sister to help."

"I'm headed out for the night," Nurse Grey said. "Angie Smalls will take the night shift if you need anything. She'll come to take the baby back to the nursery when you're ready to sleep." She turned to Jenna. "I take it you're Miss Berry's sister?"

Jenna nodded, too shocked to form words.

"They brought Miss Berry in so quickly I'm sure there's paperwork to sign in admissions. Now would be a good time to take care of that while the baby is feeding."

"Yes, of course." Jenna stood.

"Goodnight, ladies," Nurse Grey said with a smile.

"Goodnight, and thank you," Brittany said. "For everything."

"Congratulations, Miss Berry," the nurse said. "She's a beautiful baby."

A younger nurse entered the room. "Oh, Lena, you're still here?"

Nurse Grey nodded. "Just on my way out. I need to get home to make sure Mama gets her meds."

"How is your mama," the young nurse asked as she took the baby from Brittany and laid her in the bassinet.

Nurse Grey's lips pressed together. "She doesn't remember me at all."

"Nurse Grey's mother has Alzheimer's," Brittany said.

"I'm so sorry," Jenna said. "It has to be hard."

Nurse Grey nodded. "No one really prepares for this—mentally or financially." She shrugged. "Life is full circle. She cared for me when I couldn't care for myself as an infant and child. It's my turn to care for her when she can't care for herself. Speaking of which…I'm outta here."

The older nurse left.

"Do you want me to take the baby to the nursery?" Nurse Smalls asked.

"Not yet," Brittany said. "I want my sister to get to know her a little better."

"Buzz me if you or the baby need anything. I need to check on the other new mothers." Nurse Smalls left the room.

"I have to run by admissions first," Jenna said. "Will you be awake long enough for me to get there and back?"

Brittany yawned again. "I will."

Jenna shot a worried glance at Brittany. "Will you be all right alone with the baby?"

Brittany draped an arm over the side of the bassinet and stroked the baby's cheek. "I'll be okay. She's asleep. I can stay awake until you get back. I want you to get to know your niece before we descend on your little cottage."

Jenna hadn't thought past the idea that she had a niece to even consider taking her sister and the baby home. Her little three-bedroom-one-bathroom cottage had been all she'd needed when she'd come to live there and had taken the job of regional agent for the tiny FBI outpost.

The addition of one more adult and an infant... well, they'd just have to make do. Jenna wouldn't say no to her sister and the baby in their time of need. No matter how many times she'd bailed Brittany out of financial and relationship disasters, she was the only family she had left. Her lips lifted as she stared down at the tiny baby. Okay, so now, Brittany and her baby were the only two members of her family she had left.

"I'll hurry," Jenna promised and slipped out of the room, letting the door swing closed softly behind her.

Angie Smalls, carrying a Styrofoam cup with a straw, turned a smile her way as she entered a room several doors down from Brittany's.

Jenna passed a slim young man wearing a gray maintenance coverall with a hospital ID card dangling from a clip on his pocket. He carried a wad of sheets to a large canvas laundry basket on wheels and dumped them inside before ducking into one of the rooms.

A heavily pregnant woman in a hospital gown and bright yellow hospital-issue socks leaned against a man as they walked the length of the hallway. She stopped, curled her arm around her huge belly and bent over. "That was a good one."

The man glanced at his watch. "The contractions are coming faster. Not long now." He rubbed her back a few times and whispered, "Have I told you how beautiful you look?"

She snorted, the sound cut off as she doubled over again. "Yeah, right," she hissed. "Shut up and get me back to the room."

"Yes, ma'am," the man said with a grin.

Jenna shook her head. Delivering a baby wasn't

for the faint of heart. Based on the woman's expression, the pain was significant.

Brittany had gone through labor and delivery without someone she knew and loved. She couldn't blame her for wanting to keep her baby girl. After nine months carrying her and a traumatic delivery, she had to have developed feelings for the little being.

Jenna took the elevator down to the first floor and stopped at the admissions desk, where she filled out paperwork, wondering how much having a baby cost. Since Brittany didn't have a job and wasn't one to think too far ahead, Jenna would bet she didn't have insurance.

She signed the papers and squared her shoulders, knowing she'd be the one to wade through the bureaucracy to get the baby covered under Medicaid or any option available until Brittany could find a job or go back to college or a trade school.

Whatever choice Brittany made, she couldn't go off half-cocked. She had a baby to consider. Her days of being a rolling stone were over.

Jenna shook her head as she headed for the elevator. She wasn't sure Brittany would rise to the challenge of being a mother to that sweet little infant, which meant her big sister would have to make sure the baby was cared for properly. They'd also have to come up with the money to pay back the man who'd funded Brittany during the last weeks of her pregnancy.

In the meantime, Jenna had to get her home ready for Brittany and her infant daughter. Didn't babies need a lot of stuff like a crib, diapers, bottles and so much more?

Jenna's gut clenched. More than likely, she'd help Brittany care for the babe. She wasn't ready to take on a newborn. What did she know about babies?

Nothing.

Holy hell. Her simple, single life just got a whole lot more complicated.

Back up the elevator to the third floor, Jenna breathed in and out, willing her heartbeat to slow before she had a full-blown panic attack.

Having an infant in her house would take some getting used to, but she could do it.

As the elevator reached the third floor, Jenna drew in a deep breath and let it out slowly. The doors parted, and she stepped out.

The hallway was empty except for the janitor in the gray coverall at the far end, pushing a large yellow mop bucket through the door to the stairwell.

Jenna pasted a smile on her face and strode toward Brittany's room. She could do this.

They could do this.

Together.

Before she reached the door, it swung open.

"Help!" Brittany clung to the door, blood dripping from a wound on her temple. She spotted Jenna and lurched toward her. "Help! Oh, dear God. Help!"

She fell into Jenna's arms.

Jenna staggered backward, taking her sister's full weight. "What's wrong?"

"My baby," Brittany cried. "He stole my baby!"

Jenna's heart thudded against her ribs. "The baby?" She steadied Brittany and held her at arm's length. "Where's the baby?"

Tears streamed from her eyes. "The janitor. He came into my room while I was in the bathroom. When I came out, he was leaning over the bassinet. I...I asked him what the hell..." She shook her head from side to side. "He grabbed my dinner tray and came at me...and hit me." She touched a hand to her temple, coming away with blood. "I fell, but he kept hitting me. I...must've blacked out. When I got up, he was gone..." Brittany stared into Jenna's eyes. "And so was my baby. You have to catch him."

Jenna remembered seeing the janitor pushing a mop bucket through the stairwell door. She hadn't seen the man's face. "What did he look like?"

"I don't know. One moment he had his back to me, and the next, he was pounding me with the tray."

"Was he young? Old? Facial hair?"

"I...I..." Tears slipped down Brittany's cheeks. "Can't remember. Maybe a mustache? I mostly remember the tray coming at me. Then he was gone." Her breath caught. "With my baby. Go after him!" Brittany pushed away from Jenna. "Go before he gets away."

She swayed and would have fallen if Jenna hadn't stepped forward and wrapped an arm around her. "I can't leave you like this."

"I don't care about me," Brittany cried. "Save my baby!"

Angie Smalls, the nurse on the night shift, emerged from a room down the hallway, a frown creasing her brow. "What's going on?" She rushed forward. "What are you doing up?"

"Did anyone come to collect my sister's baby?" Jenna asked, hoping Brittany was wrong and this was all a mistake, though her gut told her it wasn't.

Angie shook her head. "I didn't. She said she wanted to keep her in the room a little longer." Her brow dipped. "Why?"

"She's gone," Brittany sobbed. "He took her." She pushed away from Jenna. "Find him. Find my baby." When she staggered backward, the nurse slid an arm around her.

Jenna met the nurse's gaze. "Take care of her. I'm going after the man who took the baby."

"I'll call security. They'll lock down the hospital until the baby's found." Angie, hampered by supporting Brittany's waist, moved toward the nurses' station.

Jenna ran to the far end of the hallway and burst through the door. The janitor had a head start on her. Would it be too much of a lead for her to catch him before he left the hospital?

She didn't know, but she did know she had to try.
Her baby niece's life depended on it.

ABOUT THE AUTHOR

ELLE JAMES also writing as MYLA JACKSON is a *New York Times* and *USA Today* Bestselling author of books including cowboys, intrigues and paranormal adventures that keep her readers on the edges of their seats. When she's not at her computer, she's traveling, snow skiing, boating, or riding her ATV, dreaming up new stories. Learn more about Elle James at www.ellejames.com

Website | Facebook | Twitter | GoodReads | Newsletter | BookBub | Amazon

Or visit her alter ego Myla Jackson at mylajackson.com
Website | Facebook | Twitter | Newsletter

Follow Me!
www.ellejames.com
ellejamesauthor@gmail.com

ALSO BY ELLE JAMES

Gerard (#2)

Lucas (#3)

Beau (#4)

Rafael (#5)

Valentin (#6)

Landry (#7)

Simon (#8)

Maurice (#9)

Jacques (#10)

Brotherhood Protectors Yellowstone

Saving Kyla (#1)

Saving Chelsea (#2)

Saving Amanda (#3)

Saving Liliana (#4)

Saving Breely (#5)

Saving Savvie (#6)

Saving Jenna (#7)

Saving Peyton (#8)

Saving Londyn (#9)

Brotherhood Protectors Colorado

SEAL Salvation (#1)

Rocky Mountain Rescue (#2)

Ranger Redemption (#3)

Breaking Silence (#1)

Breaking Rules (#2)

Breaking Away (#3)

Breaking Free (#4)

Breaking Hearts (#5)

Breaking Ties (#6)

Breaking Point (#7)

Breaking Dawn (#8)

Breaking Promises (#9)

Hearts & Heroes Series

Wyatt's War (#1)

Mack's Witness (#2)

Ronin's Return (#3)

Sam's Surrender (#4)

Hellfire Series

Hellfire, Texas (#1)

Justice Burning (#2)

Smoldering Desire (#3)

Hellfire in High Heels (#4)

Playing With Fire (#5)

Up in Flames (#6)

Total Meltdown (#7)

Take No Prisoners Series

SEAL's Honor (#1)

SEAL'S Desire (#2)

SEAL's Embrace (#3)

SEAL's Obsession (#4)

SEAL's Proposal (#5)

SEAL's Seduction (#6)

SEAL'S Defiance (#7)

SEAL's Deception (#8)

SEAL's Deliverance (#9)

SEAL's Ultimate Challenge (#10)

Texas Billionaire Club

Tarzan & Janine (#1)

Something To Talk About (#2)

Who's Your Daddy (#3)

Love & War (#4)

Billionaire Online Dating Service

The Billionaire Husband Test (#1)

The Billionaire Cinderella Test (#2)

The Billionaire Bride Test (#3)

The Billionaire Daddy Test (#4)

The Billionaire Matchmaker Test (#5)

The Billionaire Glitch Date (#6)

The Billionaire Perfect Date (#7)

Warrior's Conquest

Enslaved by the Viking Short Story

Conquests

Smokin' Hot Firemen

Protecting the Colton Bride

Protecting the Colton Bride & Colton's Cowboy Code

Heir to Murder

Secret Service Rescue

High Octane Heroes

Haunted

Engaged with the Boss

Cowboy Brigade

An Unexpected Clue

Under Suspicion, With Child

Texas-Size Secrets

Made in the USA
Monee, IL
27 August 2024

64677986R00151